WHEN THE DUST SETTLES

Sabrina Johnson Fye

DEDICATION

In loving Memory of Mr. Stanley Cecilo Thomas
Just as I was about to release this book you gained
your wings…
Love you always

CHAPTER ONE

"This mom's night out is so long overdue," whispered Monica.

"Girl, yes, I'm so glad that we could get together. Between husbands, jobs and babies, our girl time has been limited," Lisa whispered back.

About twenty minutes into the movie, Monica's phone began to vibrate non-stop. She tried to ignore it, but it became annoying for everyone.

"Let me ease out and get this... Something must be wrong. I hope it's not my baby," she whispered to Lisa.

"Okay girl, go get it."

Monica quickly tiptoed out and answered the phone. The voice on the other end wasn't her mother's, but it was instantly recognizable!

"Monica! Monica, thank God you answered," said the voice on the other end. It was Bryan. The way he said her name made her heart leap into her throat.

"Oh hey, Bryan—what's wrong?"

"Monica … it's Nigel. You need to get to Wesley Memorial right now!"

Monica suddenly felt as if she was getting light-headed.

"Please don't tell me my husband is dead! What happened, what happened to him?" she yelled frantically.

"No hun, he's not dead but it's serious. We need you here now! There was an accident, he was stabbed…"

"Bryan, what *happened* to my husband? Tell me, now!"

"Okay! We were called out to a bar fight. Two drunks were fighting, we broke it up and arrested both of them. I had my guy in handcuffs, walking him out, when I heard Nigel yell. The older brother was upset because his little brother got his butt whipped and he was going to jail! He took it out on Nigel. He stabbed him in the back! I pushed my guy to the floor and ran back to him. I couldn't do anything but call for help! Honey, you need to get here now! Can you drive, are you okay to drive? Are you alone? Monica?"

Monica stood speechless, as she tried to process it all.

"Monica, Monica—are you okay?"

"Yes, I'm alright, I'm on the way!"

Part of her wanted to leave immediately, but her things were inside and she really felt too weak to drive. So she ran back into the dark theater to get her friend, ranting as she grabbed her purse and drink.

"Lisa! Lisa, come on, we need to *go*!"

"What's wrong?" asked Lisa.

"It's Nigel! Nigel has been stabbed and it sounds serious! Can you take me to the hospital? I don't think I can drive."

"Yes, girl, let's go," Lisa agreed, springing into action.

Lisa drove nervously trying to get Monica to Wesley Memorial, which was 10 miles away. For some odd reason, it seemed as if every downtown traffic light stopped them.

While sitting at the traffic light, Monica closed her eyes and prayed. She rocked back and forth, as she cried out to God. When she opened her eyes, she was surprised to see a patrol car beside them, in the next lane. The officer was waving, trying to get her attention. He gestured for her to let her window down.

"Excuse me, ma'am, are you Monica?" he asked.

"Yes," she replied reluctantly.

"Monica, I'm Officer Reynolds, a friend of your husband's. Put on your flashers and follow me!"

Monica agreed, nodding.

With his lights flashing and sirens blaring, Officer Reynolds raced them to the hospital. The parking lot was full of patrol cars.

"OMG, look at all of the patrol cars! Dear God, please don't let him be dead!" Monica exclaimed.

"Don't think like that, Monica! Pull yourself together, here comes the officer,"

said Lisa.

3

Officer Reynolds helped Monica out of the car and walked her into the ICU waiting room. Every officer in the room stood at the sight of her entering.

"Has the doctor come out yet?" she asked.

"Not yet," replied Chief Myers.

Several on and off duty officers anxiously waited for the doctor's report on the status of Nigel's condition. Suddenly, the double doors opened. It was Dr. Allen, the attending doctor!

"Monica Henderson—I'm looking for Mrs. Monica Henderson," he announced.

"Yes, sir, I'm Mrs. Henderson, Nigel's wife. How is he doing, doc?"

"He'll be okay, the knife missed all of the vital organs. However, there is a possibility that it may have severed his spine. He has a lot of swelling right now and it's not very clear. At this moment we would say that it severed only a portion of the spine. We'd like to wait until some of the swellings have gone down before making a final diagnosis."

"Can I see him?" Monica asked, crying.

"Well, he is in recovery right now. Give him a couple of hours and I'll have a nurse come to get you."

"Thank you, Dr. Allen," said Monica.

As soon as the doctor left the area, Michael, Nigel's brother, gathered everyone for prayer.

"Merciful Father, we thank you for sparing my brother's life. We thank you for guiding the hands of surgeons and for things being as well as they are. We ask that you will be his strength on the road ahead. Strengthen Monica's mind, body, and soul for the challenge she's about to face. Bless us all to be supportive in every way. Amen."

Eventually, most of Nigel's co-workers returned to work. Only the Chief and a few others stayed with Monica throughout the night. She made Bryan go over the incident over and over again. She struggled with trying to process it. However, one thing that she knew for sure was that she had to pull herself together before she saw him.

If there was anybody that could read her, it was her husband. In the wee hours of the morning, the nurse escorted Monica to see Nigel. Bryan went with her. The sight of him lying there, so helplessly, was almost more than she could take. She quickly turned, buried her head in Bryan's chest, and silently wept. Quickly, she pulled herself together, turned around, dried her eyes and tried it again.

"Baby? Baby, can you hear me? It's Monica," she began, holding his hand.

"Mmmm...Mon," he moaned. He was too weak to open his eyes. He just laid there and blinked. Monica noticed that there was no grip or strength in his hand. It was limp.

"What's wrong with his hand?" she asked.

"I don't know," Bryan responded.

"Bryan—get the doctor," she commanded.

Bryan immediately went to the nurse's station looking for him. Dr. Allen happened to be sitting at the desk.

"Excuse me, can you come into the room? My partner's wife has some questions," said Bryan.

The doctor followed Bryan back into the room and closed the door.

"What's wrong ma'am, I understand you wanted to talk to me?"

"Yes, come look at this, Dr. Allen," Monica said, picking up his hand, which fell limply back onto the bed. "What's wrong with his hand?"

"Well, ma'am, remember that temporary condition that we decided to wait and discuss?" The doctor pointed to Nigel, gesturing that he could hear them. Then, he signaled for them to follow him out into the hallway.

"Mrs. Henderson, minimum swellings have gone down," he continued once they were outside. "However, we can see that due to the damage to his spine, he is now paralyzed from the neck down. Hopefully, it's only temporary. We will know more as the swellings go down and the pressure is off the nerve. We are looking for the situation to change. However, I'd like to remind you that the spine is one big bundle of nerves, and nerves heal slowly."

"He *will* walk again, right? Please tell me there's a chance," Bryan pleaded.

"Still too soon to say," Doctor Allen responded.

Monica was totally in shock. She wasn't sure how much more she could take! They reentered the room and Bryan escorted her to a seat. She couldn't believe it! Only four years on the force and he'd been hurt. Thank God, he was still alive! A new baby, a new condo, and a quadriplegic husband! *Lord, what am I going to do?* She thought as she sat, staring at her husband in disbelief.

"Monica hun, are you alright?" Bryan enquired, concerned.

She nodded. "Yeah, I think I'm going to step out and let some of his family come in to see him." She hurried down the hallway and out into the lobby. All eyes were on her as she broke down in tears before making it to the nearest seat. Everyone ran to her side.

"What's happened? Monica! Dear Lord, my child," cried out Nigel's mom in anguish.

"Monica! Monica," cried her own mom, as she made her way through the cluster of people.. She sat down in the seat beside her daughter. "Lord, please help my child," she cried, holding Monica's hand.

Her sobbing and weeping pierced the hearts of everyone in the room. Even Chief Myers was fighting back the tears.

"Monica, what did they say? How's my son?" demanded his mother frantically.

"My husband, my poor husband is a quad! I don't know how he's going to handle this," Monica wailed, falling limp into her mother's arms.

"A quadriplegic?" his mom repeated in disbelief.

"Yes ma'am," Monica replied, in tears.

"Call Pastor Richards," Monica's mother mouthed to Lisa.

Lisa made the call, then went back to the condo to pack a bag for Monica.

Later, Monica made herself as comfortable as possible on the little couch in the room with her husband. She laid there in the dark trying to comprehend the day. What happened to their lives, and how did things change so drastically in one day? Would it ever be the same, she pondered. The whole day seemed like one big nightmare, one that she couldn't wait to end! Only this wasn't a dream.

The next day, Dr. Allen made his rounds. *I hope he's going to break the news to him, because I can't*, thought Monica.

When the doctor entered the room Nigel was still medicated.

"Just came in to check on him and do a few tests," he announced as he walked in and began to uncover Nigel. Unfortunately, he woke him up.

"Hey doc," he growled.

Monica moved quickly to his bedside. He turned his head and smiled.

"Hey, Mon,"

"Hi honey," she replied.

"Doc, I can't feel my body, everything's numb!"

"Okay, give me a few seconds..." The doctor logged some information into the computer.

"Monica! Monica baby, grab my hand," Nigel hissed.

"Maybe we should wait until Dr. Allen is finished, babe," she whispered.

"Monica, *now*!" he demanded.

Reluctantly, she took his hand in hers and squeezed.

"Are you squeezing, baby?"

Monica nodded yes.

"I swear, I can't feel a *thing*! I can't move, it's like I have no body!"

"Mr. Henderson, you've had a very traumatic injury and right now you have paralysis due to the trauma."

"Paralysis! I'm *paralyzed*? My whole body?" asked Nigel, in disbelief. "Oh God, no! *Please*, God! Lord, I can't move!"

He began to cry and sob like a baby, pleading to God. "Lord, what am I going to do? Lord, my wife, my baby, my job!"

His crying, pleading, and desperation was more than Monica could take. Rivers of tears coursed down her face as she leaned in, trying to console her husband.

"It's going to be okay, babe. I'm right here. God's got us, we are going to be *fine*."

"I can't move, baby. I can't do anything! I'm like a baby!

You're my wife and I'm no good to you." Nigel closed his eyes.

"That's not true, I love you, honey..." Monica replied.

"Jesus, please, I can't live like this…"

Dr. Allen gestured to his nurse to give him something to calm him down.

"Mr. Henderson, your body just needs time to heal. I don't want to misdiagnose your condition. However, I am praying and truly believe that you will regain upper body mobility." As he spoke the nurse squeezed the morphine pump, which put Nigel to rest within seconds.

"I'm going to leave the two of you. I will check on you again tomorrow."

"Thank you, doctor," said Monica.

Feeling empathetic, he nodded and exited the room.

Monica laid her head on her husband's chest and cried for a long time.

The word was out! The next day around noon, their phones became a hotline. People were calling; family, friends and church members.

Shortly afterwards, his mom arrived with Pastor James. She had called him in for Nigel, but actually, she needed him for support as well. His father joined them shortly.

"Hello, son," said Pastor James as he stood at Nigel's bedside.

Exhausted and slightly drugged, Nigel cracked his eyes open, and peered out long enough to recognize his mom, the pastor Richards zxand his father, who was also a pastor.

"Pastor," he managed, shaking his head from side to side, "I'm a vegetable!" He wasn't able to shed another tear. He and Monica both had cried so much, their eyes were swollen.

"Why me, dad? I don't understand!" he said looking to his dad for answers.

"I don't know, son, sometimes we don't always have the answers. But one thing is for sure: God is faithful. He promised to never leave us nor forsake us, and he promised to never put more on us than we can bear." The pastor in him spoke him, his father's heart was being ripped apart. It made his heart ache to see his son in this condition.

His father also gave words of faith, that brought some comfort. Yet once his parents left, Nigel was back into the battle with his reality. The next few days were extremely rough for him. He fell into depression.

CHAPTER TWO

"Hey, baby, good morning to you! Give me a kiss," said Monica as she leaned over the bed and kissed his face.

"What's so good about it?" he asked, with his recently-acquired surliness.

"The fact that you are alive, I'm leaning over your bed looking into those eyes. The eyes that I fell in love with..."

"I hope you still love them, because they're all that I have left!" He snapped.

"Okay, no! Let me tell you something, Nigel Maurice Henderson. I will *not* sit here day after day, while you slip into your pity parties. I love you! NJ needs his daddy, and you will *no*t give up! I need you to fight for your family!"

"How can I fight, baby, and I can't move?"

"You *can* fight, in your mind! You do know that the battlefield is in your mind, right? Come on, honey, you're a preacher's kid ... you know The Word! You will speak life and not death! So, I'm telling you right now that you *will* get out of this bed! But until you do, I'm going to be right here, in it with you!"

Monica let down the rail of the bed and crawled in, right on top of him.

"Now, you just lay right here and hold me just like you do every night. Hold me in your mind, babe. If you do it in your mind, your body will soon follow, you watch! Do you hear me?"

"Yes, baby, I hear you," Nigel replied in a low voice.

"Are you holding me?" she asked, as she laid her head on his chest.

"Yes, baby, I'm holding you." Unable to hold back his tears, Nigel silently wept as she laid on his chest. Looking up and seeing his tears, she wiped them away and kissed his face.

"Don't worry, baby, one day when we're old, we're going to think about this and share with our children and grandchildren this testimony of the goodness of God. All I can say is, if you truly love me, you'll fight for me, for us, for our family. Only a coward would give up his family without a fight. You, my friend, are definitely no coward! You are one of the strongest men that I know. Come on baby, tap into that Aries stubborn, goat-headed mentality!"

"Aye aye, captain" Nigel responded, smiling. "Okay, babe. You have my word, I *will* fight!"

When the doctor came back around to visit, he was surprised to see Monica in the bed with her husband. Both of them were fast asleep.

"Oh look, I'll wake her," volunteered the nurse.

"No, don't," said Dr. Allen. "According to his vitals and monitors, this is the best rest he's had since the surgery. Rest is what he needs right now. She's not directly laying on him, so it's fine. Please tell her to be mindful not to pull out his catheter. Let them rest."

Later, Monica was awakened by the movement of the nurse trying to check Nigel's vitals.

"Good morning, or should I say, good afternoon, Mrs. Henderson. It looks like both of you got some well-needed rest." Realizing that she was still in her husband's bed, Monica felt self-conscious.

"Oh my, I'm sorry," she began, trying to struggle out of his bed. It's just that he's having a real emotional time right now …"

"Don't worry about it ma'am, it's perfectly okay. The doctor was in this morning, he stopped us from waking you. Mr. Henderson needs rest to heal. If it takes you being in the bed with him, then that's fine. The doctor just asked me to remind you that he has a catheter; be careful and try not to pull it out."

"Yes, thank you. I will be mindful of it," agreed Monica gratefully. "Nurse, before you leave, I must ask. How long do you think it will be before his upper body regains feeling?"

"No one can say, but I can definitely tell you that staying calm and getting rest is really essential". By now, Nigel was wide awake and listening to their conversation. He sighed deeply.

"Monica, leave these people alone. This is something that we couldn't rush or speed up even if we wanted to."

"Well, praise God—I'm glad to hear you say something positive!"

"We just gotta wait, baby, that's all I'm trying to say."

"Yes, honey, you are right. I won't ask them again," she replied.

"But since you are awake, Nigel, you know I haven't been home in days. I need to go home, shower, repack my bag and see about NJ for a little while. I will be back before supper tonight, okay? Bryan should be here in a little bit."

"Sure baby, I understand. Go ahead, I will be fine. Although I'm not really in the mood for company."

"*Company*? Bryan's not company! He's your partner, NJ's godfather—he's family! It would also be good for him to see you in high spirits. He needs to see that you're okay. He's been blowing up my phone five times a day. It's not safe for him to be on the beat with you on his mind. It's too distracting."

"Yeah, you're right … as always," said Nigel sarcastically.

"Thank you, and don't you forget it!" she answered quickly, grinning.

"Hey there, partner," said Bryan as he entered the room. It was so hard for him to see his partner and his best friend lying so helplessly there on his back. "What's going on tough guy, how are you feeling today?"

"Shoot, definitely not tough!" Nigel admitted.

"Yeah well, one day at a time, man, one day at a time. Everybody's praying for you. Guess what, in your honor, the whole precinct is filled with that stinking black licorice that you like. There's a little jar of it on each desk! Nobody's eating that crap, of course, it's nasty!"

Nigel smiled. "No, it's good, and it's good *for* you. It also has medicinal properties."

"Well, when you get back, we're going to have a truckload of it for you!" laughed Bryan.

"Stop it, dude, you know I ain't ever coming back, man."

"No, *you* listen," said Bryan, speaking sternly to his best friend. "You have to fight—you gotta *want* this, Nigel! I know it's hard, it's hard for all of us! Just know that we are here for you! We can't fight for you, but we definitely can fight with you! You told me you wanted to be a police officer ever since you were five years old. So now you've been out there and you've had a major setback. But it doesn't mean that it's over! I mean, these doctors are good. I don't mean any disrespect, but they ain't God! Whose report shall you believe?"

"I know bro, but while I'm lying here, all I can do is think. Do you know what type of burden I'm going to be on my wife and my family? I'll have to watch Monica do everything! We have bills … I can't help. We have a child and I can't help with him either. Heck, she's even going to be changing my diapers for a little while!" He sighed, fighting back the tears.

"You know what, man, you're right. The only thing that you forgot to mention is that she would do it all with love! That woman loves you! Everything that you just said was correct and it's going to remain your reality if you don't *do* something about it. Pray, believe, fight and push through it! You aren't fighting by yourself. Don't worry about the money right now. Your brothers are turning in PTO time by the dozens."

"What?"

"Yes, I asked the Chief if I could give you some of my PTO time. I normally sell it back anyway. He said yes. I had no idea that he was going to ask the fellows to do the same. Man, at the end of the briefing the numbers were still going up! I think he's even reached out to the west side precinct. Everyone was overjoyed. It's the least that we can do. So ease your mind, stop worrying about money right now. Monica is going to be fine. When she tells you about this, you better act surprised!"

"I don't know how to thank y'all, man."

"Thank us by fighting for your life! I know it hasn't been long and is a lot to process, but get your mind in the right place. We got your back!"

"Thanks, bro."

"Good, now let's talk about something else."

A familiar voice broke the fog of emotions.

"Knock, knock, knock!" It was Nigel's mom and dad.

"Ha, mom and pops," Bryan greeted them. "Look, Nigel, I'm going to cut my visit a little short, bro. I'm going to let the folks stay here with you for a while. Remember what I told you!"

"Yes, yes, thank you, man. I love you, bro, you're a good man."

"Thanks, I try," said Bryan, laughing.

This time Nigel's mom was prepared to see her son. She came prayed up! Equipped with markers, index cards, and her Bible! She was ready to pour some faith into her son. "How's mama's big man today?" she asked.

Nigel smiled. "That's what you called me when I was a little boy and I got sick."

"Well, no matter how old you are, mister, you'll always be my big man."

"Yes, ma'am, you're right."

They stayed for a while, giving Monica a well-deserved break. Nigel's mom wrote healing scriptures and taped them to the walls in his room. She stood in the chair and taped them as high as she could reach. Of course Nigel and his dad tried to convince her that standing in the chair wasn't a good idea, but what can you do with a determined woman! She made him promise that he and Monica would recite them together, every day!

Nigel's progress seemed to be slow. Eventually, he was transferred from the hospital to a rehabilitation facility where he received therapy. Early one morning before dawn, Monica was awakened by his moans.

"Nigel, what's wrong?" She asked.

"Ummm ... baby, can you switch sides? You're lying on my arm," he whispered.

Still half-asleep, Monica wiggled to adjust herself. As soon as she was comfortable, she realized that he could feel!

"Wait," she said, snatching back the covers and leaning into his face. "Baby, wake *up*! How did you know that I was laying on your arm?"

"Because it's tingling—you're cutting off my circulation," Nigel whispered, still half-asleep.

"I swear I'm married to a Saint Bernard. Did you wet my shirt with your drool?"

Frantically, Monica searched his chest with her hand: it was soaked! She was so happy; without thinking she kissed him, right on the mouth, morning breath and all!

"Nurse, *nurse*!" she yelled, pressing the call button as she slid out of the bed. She pressed the call button again with desperation, still no answer!

"Shoot!" she said, swiftly pushing her feet in her slippers and racing for the door.

"Excuse me! Excuse me!" she called as she ran towards the nurses' station.

"Yes ma'am, what's wrong, Mrs. Henderson?"

"It's my husband Nigel! I think he just regained feeling in his upper body! He even knew that I drooled on his shirt!" she gushed, happily!

"Okay, we have an emergency down the hall. Please give us a few minutes and someone will be right in."

"Sure, okay, thanks," Monica responded, running back to be with her husband.

"Baby, are you asleep?" she asked, flipping on the lights of Nigel's room.

"Nope."

"Good, because someone's on the way to check you out. They had an emergency down the hall. Let me wash our faces before they get here."

She ran to the sink and wet a washcloth. First she washed her face, then his. She anxiously awaited their arrival. Nurses Amber and Latoya came into the room carrying equipment. Nigel had been there so long, the staff felt like family.

"Okay, Mr. Henderson."

"Nigel," he corrected her.

"Alright, Nigel. Come on, let's see what's happening here. The wife thinks we're regaining feeling. Can you tell me what's going on?" she questioned.

"Sure, well, I was asleep. Then I felt my arm tingling like someone was sticking pins in it. I could feel a heaviness on my arm and my chest felt wet. That's when I realized my Saint Bernard was laying on me." He looked at Monica smiling, as she gave him the "I got you" eye. The nurses laughed.

"Well, in that case, pup—I mean Monica, let me get over there, please, so I can check him out," laughed Amber.

"Okay, Nigel—come on, give me a good reason to call your doctor and wake him up! Can you squeeze my fingers?"

"No," he replied, and Monica's heart dropped. "… but I *can* feel you touching my hand."

"Great, I'll take that! Now, tell me if you feel this..." She took a cool swab and traced it down his arm.

"Yep, yep, I can feel it! That's cold, am I right?" he asked, fishing for hope.

"Yes sir, you are so right! Now, let's check your sensitivity in your neck and your chest."

This time she used a small light that radiated heat.

"Oh my, that's a little warm," commented Nigel.

Monica began jumping up and down and clapping! Then she found herself with her hands lifted high, giving God all the praise.

"Awesome, Mr. Henderson! Still a ways to go, but you've made major progress! I'm going to call the doctor. I'm sure he'll be here first thing in the morning," said Latoya.

"Congratulations. I'll send a dry gown for you, and a bib for you know who…" smiled Amber.

"No, no need to send someone. I can manage, fresh gowns are in the cabinet," Monica pointed out.

Again, the nurses laughed as Monica peered into Nigel's face with an evil eye! As soon as they left the room, she showered him with kisses. She planted kisses all over his face.

"I told you, I *told* you, baby! I told you that we would be alright!"

"Yes, you did … but you heard her say that I still have a long way to go."

"No, the only thing I heard was, but God! But God shall supply all of our needs … right now, we need for you to get out of this bed! Praise God, He's doing it. Slowly, but surely … He's doing it! It ain't over until *God* says it's over! He Is A Healer!"

"Now, let us pray: "Our heavenly father, once again you have heard our cry! We thank you for this progress. I see complete healing and I thank you in advance for letting my husband walk again, in Jesus' name. Amen! Oh yeah and just so you know, that Saint Bernard joke is going to bite you in the butt! You just wait and see," said Monica, as she settled under Nigel's arm.

"Come on babe, it was a joke. You've been trying to make me laugh for weeks."

"Calm down, I'm not mad, but I *will* get you back," she laughed.

Monica gave him one more good night peck and they rested until the doctor came in the next morning.

"Rise and shine, lovebirds!" He announced himself into the room, flipping on the lights.

"A little bird told me that you are making progress, looks like you're on your way. Good morning ma'am," he addressed Monica, as she scurried out of the bed.

"Yes sir, I am, thanks to God, prayer and my wife, by my side!"

"Great, keep thinking like that. I'm going to turn you over and take a look at your wound ... well, it seems to be healing nicely. The swelling in the area has gone down tremendously. I know that's one of the reasons sensitivity is coming back. Keep doing whatever you're doing!"

"Thanks, doc, do you know when I can go home?"

"Let's just give it six more weeks. The swelling will have gone down a bit more and it will give me a chance to get some assistance set up for you and your family."

"Okay, six weeks it is! I can't wait to see my baby boy! I don't want him to come in here and see me like this."

"I understand. I also think that it's time that we start getting you up. You'll be in the reclining chair most of the day. It will help to strengthen your back."

"Yes sir, whatever you say, to keep my progress going!"

Monica could not wait to tell Bryan and the family the news.

CHAPTER THREE

amily, friends and co-workers were calling and stopping by to see for themselves. Everyone rejoiced in his improvement! For the first time in a long time, Monica saw a glimpse of life in her husband's face again. She was so happy, she couldn't fight back the tears. Crying was the one thing that Nigel could not stand to see her do.

"Hey, hey girl, don't cry! Please don't cry, baby," he begged.

"I can't help it. Besides, these are tears of joy, so don't worry." She leaned in and kissed his face.

"Please don't give up on me. I'm on my way back, Mon. I'm fighting like you asked. But just know I can't do this without you."

"Now don't you worry about that, because you won't ever have to. I'm so proud of you, babe."

Just as she leaned in for another kiss, her phone rang.

"It's my job," she said.

"Hello Monica, this is Amanda." She quickly turned and walked a few steps away from him. His eyes and ears were glued to her every word.

"Hey Mandy, what's up?"

"Girl, I hate to bother you with this, but HR just called and you are out of leave time and the time that we gave you. They're requesting that you return on Monday."

"Really, Nigel is just starting to show some improvement, but I knew that I didn't have forever. I'll be there."

"How is he?" asked Mandy.

"He's doing well." Monica turned back around to smile at him, while giving Amanda the update.

"Well that's awesome, tell him to keep up the good work, and we will see you Monday."

"Okay, see you then."

"Monica, what's going on?" asked Nigel the minute she hung up.

"Stop worrying! You only call me Monica when you're mad or worried! That was Amanda. HR called, they want me to return on Monday. I guess our little man will be going to daycare. Therefore, I'm going to have to leave and take care of a few things. I'll see you tonight."

"Okay, go, I'm fine. Kiss my boy for me."

Monica quickly left for the daycare, to set up arrangements for her son's return.

As she drove, she realized it was almost 6 p.m. and a daycare would be closed by the time she got there. She decided to pull over and call instead.

Ms. Deborah answered and Monica explained her situation.

"Mrs. Henderson, unfortunately all of the infants' rooms are full."

"You don't understand, I will be returning to work on Monday! Come on Deborah, you know me, we go to church together. Can't you make some kind of exception?"

"Sorry, Monica. I must abide by state regulations. Actually it's the best thing for everyone. We must keep our kids safe."

"Well, thanks. I'll figure out something, thank you."

Monica made several calls on the way to her mom's house. Either the daycares were too full or too expensive. Without announcing herself, she used her keys to let herself into her mom's house. As she barged through the kitchen's back door, she startled her mom and NJ. She found them eating supper while watching Wheel of Fortune. Monica threw the keys onto the counter, scooped up her baby, and took a seat at the other end of the table.

He was elated to see his mom!

"What's wrong darling, did you find him anything?"

"No ma'am, and that's the thing—I'm not used to being in this position. If Deborah would have told me months ago that she was full, I would have just taken somewhere else; no problem. Unfortunately, with Nigel in the hospital, money's tight, and bills are due! I have no wiggle room. I would have just chosen one that I liked, even if it was expensive. My emotions are all over the place right now. I hate barely making it! I hate watching my husband go through this situation, and now NJ!

"I don't mean to sound ungrateful and selfish, but it makes me mad! Mad at Nigel for taking that stupid police job! He's a certified accountant and probably would have been making more money— nope, he wouldn't listen. Following Bryan, he had to go to the academy! Now look at us!"

"Honey, I can't pretend to understand what you are going through. I also can't allow you to beat up on yourself or my son-in-law! The boy has always had yours and NJ's well-being at heart. Or have you forgotten that it was your purse getting snatched and you almost being mugged that prompted him to be a police officer? My son-in-law is a good cop and he's well respected! This was an unfortunate incident. He didn't ask for it! Now pull yourself together, look at how your baby is looking at you! He's wondering why you're crying, instead of loving him! He hasn't seen you in 2 days! For God's sake, I sure hope you're not acting like this at the facility!"

"No ma'am, never!"

"Well, I'm that glad you had this meltdown here, instead of with Nigel. God's going to work it out! Are you hungry?"

"No, ma'am."

"Okay then, give me the baby. You go upstairs, shower and get into my bed for a minute. Try to clear your mind and get a little rest."

"Okay, but I want to take NJ with me."

"Okay, I will put him to sleep and bring him to you."

"Thanks, I look forward to it. There's nothing like a nap in your mama's bed."

Doing as her mom suggested, Monica went upstairs and laid down. When she woke up it was a little after 11 o'clock. "Oh my God!" she yelled, as she fumbled for her shoes. She had to get to the hospital. It would be the last weeknight that she could sleep with Nigel. From now on, she could only stay on the weekends. *Wait, where's NJ*, she asked herself. Then she realized that her mom never meant to deliver him.

On her way out of the house, she peeped into the den to find her mother and NJ in the recliner fast asleep. She smiled. She was so lucky to have a loving, understanding mom. Not to mention how much she loved her grandson and her son-in-law. *She sure got me straight*, she thought, as the conversation replayed in her mind.

Once inside her car, she began to pray ... "Now Lord, I don't know what I'm going to do about this baby situation; but you know what, Lord? I'm not going to worry about it tonight. I'm going to the hospital and get in bed with my husband." She often had talks with God in her car. It seemed to be their meeting place. The place where she could tell him anything and she could hear him clearly.

The drive back to the hospital became short as she emptied her heart before the Lord. Before she knew it, she was in the hospital's parking lot. When she pushed his room door open, the lights were down and it was a little dark. However, a voice cried out from the darkness. "Monica?"

"Yes, it's me," she laughed as she walked in and turned on the lights above his bed. There he laid with a big grin on his face, like a little kid on his birthday.

"What's that smile for? I guess that you thought I wasn't coming back, huh?"

"I was hoping that you were, but yes, I had given up. I was thinking how stressful it's going to be for you; working, taking care of the baby and trying to see me."

"Okay, okay, stop it! I don't want to hear any more! I'll be fine," Monica insisted. "Now shush, I'm coming in!" She turned out the light, pulled back his covers and climbed in carefully. She wiggled into a nice position with her head right against his chin. She pressed in to make sure that he felt her touch.

"Do you see all of the progress that you have made in the last few weeks? We need more of that! What we don't need is for you to sit here worrying and falling into depression again. Do you know what this test has taught me, baby?"

"No, what?"

"It's taught me that I'm stronger than I ever could have imagined.

I just never needed to be strong, because I had you. Trust me, as soon as you're strong enough to relinquish your position, you can have it!"

He laughed. "Are you sure?" he asked.

"Oh my God, yes, but just know that until then, I got you!"

He laughed and said, "Come up here, so that I can kiss you."

She did as he asked.

"Do you know what I'm grateful for?" she went on. "I'm grateful for the fact that we have always been a team. The fact that you're not that selfish, all-about-me type of guy. You share your thoughts, your dreams, and fears with me, I love that about you."

"Girl, you know that you're my numero uno!"

She kissed his face as he laid there thinking.

"I just want the best for you babe, for our family! I don't want to let you or God down. I promised Him that I would take care of you."

"You have been, Nigel, and you will again! I know you will! Now, are we going to spend our last night talking, or are we going to get a little sleep?"

"Okay, but first, one more kiss. On the lips this time, please," he requested.

"I think I'll pass, I know that your lips are chapped," she teased.

He laughed. "No ma'am, they are not! I had Ava put some balm on them for me. One more kiss, Monica, come on!"

She gave him a long smack on the lips and settled back under his arm.

As soon as she was comfortable, he spoke again.

"Umm, Mon ..."

"Yes, Nigel?"

"Can you scratch my head for me?"

OMG man, for the love of God! she yelled in her mind, but dared not say it. "Sure, love," she responded instead.

As she forced herself up, he stopped her.

"I'm joking. Lay down, babe, it doesn't itch."

"Really? Come *on*, Nigel! I'm tired!"

"I'm sorry," he said, laughing. "I missed having you here all day!"

She smiled.

"Well, how about this…since I'm not sleepy I'll just lay here, quiet, and I'll listen to you sleep."

"You promise?" she asked.

"Yes ma'am, as long as you don't snore or toot."

"What?"

Monica popped out from under his arm and was now in his face again!

"Now, I admit to slightly snoring, even drooling a little bit, but I do *not* toot in my sleep."

"Monica Louise Henderson, yes ma'am, you do! We've been married for years—I should know!"

"I do not!" repeated Monica, now pouting. "It's rude and unladylike!"

"Call it what you want to, my love … it happens," he said, laughing.

"You know what? On that note, I'm getting on the couch!"

"No, don't! Wait a minute," pleaded Nigel.

"Okay, then say that I don't toot in my sleep."

"But I would be lying…" he sighed. "Okay babe, you don't toot in your sleep and I promise to stop messing with you."

Still pouting, once again she settled under his arm and began to unwind. Meanwhile, Nigel laid quietly, listening to the sound of her breathing. He could tell when she drifted asleep. "Good night, Tootie," he whispered as she slept like a baby in his arms.

Weeks went by. Monica had settled into work and NJ was being juggled between Lisa and Monica's parents. Everyone tried to help as much as they could, to avoid a daycare bill. Especially since Monica was already struggling.

Monica finally found a little rhythm in her life. She set a routine. Monday through Friday 9 to 5 she worked, Monday nights belonged to NJ and the laundry. Tuesday, Thursday and Saturday nights were Nigel's bath nights and she spent time with him. Sundays she went to church and visited for only an hour. She spent most Sunday evenings meal prepping and planning for the week. She no longer had extra money for eating out.

Everyone adapted to the routine which gradually became a new normal. One Sunday afternoon as Monica was leaving the rehab facility, she was stopped by Dr. Allen in the hallway.

"Monica! Mrs. Henderson!" he called out from the nurses' station. "Mrs. Henderson! Can I see you for a second?" He was beckoning for her to step into the corner with him, and she did so.

"No reason to be alarmed, everything is fine," Dr. Allen began. "I just wanted to talk to you about Nigel's situation."

"Situation?" Monica repeated.

"Yes, Nigel has now been at the facility for 4 months. Unfortunately, there has been little progress. I hoped that he would have been farther along by now. Nevertheless, the insurance only covers so many visits. He's getting close to the maximum days that he can stay in the facility. The way I see it is that Nigel needs to go home. I'm working on it now. He will still receive therapy three times a week. Twice at home and once here."

"Wow! How am I supposed to get him home?"

"Transit will transport him in a special van," said Dr. Allen. "I know it's a lot to take in right now. I know your plate is full and you have the baby. Do me a favor and don't mention it to Nigel just yet. I'm trying to make this as easy as possible for you. Still working out a few kinks, but in the end it will be fine. Trust me. There is a possibility that he might progress even more at home. He will be in his own environment and the baby will be a positive motivation."

"Monica stood rubbing her forehead in awe."

"So, how long do I have to prepare? When will he be released?"

"Well, I'm waiting on insurance companies to get back with me on a couple of things. So I'd like to say within about a week. If all goes well, a week from Monday."

"Jeez! Lord have mercy on me!" she shouted. "I'll get on it! Thank you, doctor."

She gave him a big hug. He seemed like a part of the family.

"Hey Monica, I want to say, through it all you have been an outstanding, dedicated wife. Every man should pray for a wife like you."

Tears filled her eyes. "Now you're going to make me cry."

"He's a lucky man, or shall I say, blessed! Now, go home and start getting ready. We have one week."

"Monday? Really? Lord, how am I going to get everything ready in a week?" she wondered sitting behind the wheel of the car. There's so much to do!

Feeling overwhelmed, she took out her frustration on the steering wheel; pounding and shaking it frantically until she was tired. She definitely needed some quality time with God!

"Dear God, Lord help me! I need your strength! It's been whirlwind after whirlwind! As soon as I adapt, here comes something else! My plate is so full! The doctor speaks about me like I'm some perfect wife, but he has no clue! Lord, I feel like a rubber band stretched to the max! If you don't help me, I will surely break! I know that you promised that you'd never put more on me than I can bear." She sat there for a moment weeping silent tears. Then the scripture "weeping may endure for a night, but joy comes in the morning" was so sweetly dropped into her spirit. She stopped crying and began to thank God in advance. "Thank you Lord, thank you for the morning. I know you will do it. I know you will see me through as always. I will give it to you! I'm casting this burden. Lord, work it out!"

Then she began to sing "He turned my mourning into dances with praise. He lifted my sorrows. I can't stay silent for the joy of the Lord has come." *There is nothing like a word from the Lord and a song when you need it,* she thought gratefully.

Monica picked up her phone and sprang into action. The first person she called was Bryan. Bryan had been such a good friend through the whole ordeal. Every day he checked on his partner and best friend. He made sure that Monica's car was washed, the grass was cut and tried to spend quality time with NJ. He was going to make some woman a great husband someday. He immediately answered her call.

"Hey Mon, anything wrong?"

"Nothing's wrong. I know you are probably just getting settled after the shift, but I couldn't wait to update you on Nigel's situation."

"What do you mean, situation? Did he move?"

"No, not yet. However, the doctor is releasing him in a week."

"What? Why?"

"It seems as if our insurance only allows coverage for a certain number of visits. So the doctor is arranging for him to have therapy here as well as at the facility. I might have to pay for some of those home sessions. I don't know how I'm going to do it, Bryan. I'm already financially strapped!"

"So, how long do we have? When is he coming home?"

"Next Monday."

"What, why so fast?"

"I don't know! All I know is that he'll be at home soon. I'm not sure if I can handle it by myself. The doctor thinks being in his home environment will motivate his progression."

"You're not alone, sis. You know that I will be there to help you anytime that you may need me, day or night."

"Thanks, Bryan, you're the best friend a guy could ask for."

"So what do you need me to do?"

"Well, first, tomorrow, I'm calling Mrs. Broussard about the vacant handicapped apartment down the street."

"Okay, let me know as soon as you hear something. Meanwhile, I'll be rallying up a few fellows to help us move."

"God bless you, Bryan, you are the *best*!"

"Go get some rest now, Monica. I'll check on you tomorrow."

Monica found a sense of peace, knowing that Bryan had her back!

Tomorrow she would have the dreaded talk with Amanda. It was inevitable! She had to have more time off!

Amazingly, Amanda was a trooper about it. She was even nice enough to give her Thursday and Friday off.

"Girl, you are a strong woman. We all admire you," said Amanda. "I know that you really need the time off. If he's still not settled in by Monday, Kim said that she'll give you two of her PTO days. Now, don't you worry. Go get your husband and bring him home."

Without much effort, things began to fall in place. There was no doubt in Monica's mind that it was God working behind the scenes.

Mrs. Broussard approved the apartment. Dr. Allen did as he promised. He had a hospital bed and other medical equipment delivered to the new apartment.

CHAPTER FOUR

It was moving day! Nigel and Monica's friends and family scrambled like ants. There was so much to do and so little time to get it done. It happened that Nigel was being dismissed on moving day, which meant that everything had to be done ASAP! His expected arrival time was 4:30. Bryan, Christian, Davis and Mark would be moving everything from the old apartment to the new handicapped apartment. Nigel couldn't have been blessed with more loyal friends.

His parents were coming over to spend the next couple of nights to help them get settled. NJ was staying with his uncle until Nigel settled in.

Monica's heart skipped a beat as the transit van came down the street. For months she was commuting back and forth to and from the rehab facility. Only God knew how much she prayed that he'd come home. Now he was finally here; just not in the condition she'd imagined. She found herself experiencing a bittersweet moment. She already prayed to God, asking him to strengthen her to be the support system that her husband needed.

Out of love and respect for Nigel, this group of tired, dedicated friends and family managed to muster enough energy to turn a grueling day into a welcome home party! They made signs from cardboard boxes saying "Welcome home, Nigel!" His buddies ordered pizza and wings. It was delivered only moments before he arrived.

Not knowing what to expect, Nigel laid there in the back of the van battling a million thoughts. *Suppose coming home was a mistake? Suppose Monica couldn't handle me and the baby? Where can I go besides a nursing home? My folks are too old to take care of me! Suppose, suppose, suppose?*

Suddenly those devil-inspired thoughts were interrupted by the sound of people yelling. The van came to a halt. Within a moment, the back doors swung open. The driver and his assistant moved in and began to pull his stretcher out. The yelling and cheering got louder! Once the structure was on the ground and stabilized he was able to turn his head to the side. He was trying to get a glimpse of what was going on! To his surprise, there they were! All of them! The most important people in his life were out there, yelling and holding up signs!

Tears began to fill his eyes! His heart was so overwhelmed!

"Man, you guys look rough!" he said, as the paramedics rolled him past the crowd and into the apartment.

Everyone laughed.

The apartment was a wreck. There were boxes everywhere! However, they managed to keep Nigel's room clean. They laid him in the hospital bed that had been delivered that morning. The other bedroom was set up for Monica and NJ. His mom was the first one to see him. His mother laid her head in his chest and wept tears of joy! Monica was next, of course. "Welcome home, baby!" she said, planting kisses on his lips.

"Monica baby, you look exhausted," observed Nigel. It ripped his heart out to see her looking so tired!

"I'm fine, I'm a big girl," she replied, intentionally smiling, trying to ease his nerves.

Honestly, she was too tired to smile. It took everything within her to put her best foot forward.

"Okay, okay … make room for the man with the plan," called Bryan, slightly nudging Monica out of the way.

Once at his bedside, Bryan reached up and began to rub Nigel's head.

"Well bro, that's all I got for you. No kisses from me!" He grabbed his friend's hand and gave it a little squeeze.

"Bryan, all I can say is thanks, man, and I love you. I could never repay you for everything that you have done for me and Monica."

"No, don't worry about it man, we're good; we're family. We're glad that you are home," Bryan assured him.

"Excuse me—now, if you two lovebirds are finished, a few of his other friends would like to see him too!" The voice was coming from the foot of the bed. It was the Chief and a couple other guys who decided to drop in for a visit. They all laughed.

"Well, on that note, I'm going to get some pizza. I'm starving," declared Bryan, still laughing as he made it across the room. They set up the party in the room with Nigel by stacking boxes against the wall. The group of tired, hungry and relieved loved ones sat along the wall, with their plates in their hands and their backs against the wall. They celebrated Nigel's return. His mom slipped out of the room without him or anyone noticing. When she returned to his bedside, she was holding a big cake in her hand.

"Mama! Is that what I *think* it is?"

"Yep, it's your favorite: chocolate on chocolate. Can you see it? It says, 'Welcome home, son!'"

"Mama, you're going to make a grown man cry. Again!"

"You'd better not! I put hard work into this cake. No one wants soggy cake!"

"I agree," Monica put in, "so let's cut it!" She took the cake from his mom, placed it on a box and proceeded to cut it. They sat until dark, eating cake and sharing silly stories about Nigel.

"I know you guys are tired. I really appreciate you all, for helping my Monica."

Their friends departed after Nigel's appreciation speech.

Both Nigel and Monica were uncomfortable with the new living arrangements and were forced to adjust to them quickly.

"Monica, how's Nigel getting along?" asked Mandy one day.

"I think he is adjusting well. He hates the fact that he can't hold NJ, but other than that, he's happy to be at home."

"We are hopeful that the doctor is right, and he'll be better soon," said Mandy.

"Yes, I hope so."

Ironically, that very same night Nigel had a breakdown. Monica had given NJ his bath. He laughed and giggled as she moisturized his skin with baby lotion. Monica enjoyed his bath time; she knew he wouldn't be that small forever. Nigel laid in his room, thinking as he listened to his family living, loving, and enjoying life without him. He too should have been on that bed tickling his son, making him and his wife laugh.

Unfortunately, there he was, lying in bed helplessly. Once again, his mind was bombarded by crazy thoughts. The devil whispered crazy things into his ear, like Monica didn't want him anymore. It was only a matter of time before she was tired of him and found NJ a real daddy.

Nigel laid there trying to pray, but he couldn't. He just began to call on the name of Jesus really loud! "Jesus, Jesus, Jesus help me, Jesus!" he prayed. His yelling startled Monica. She quickly put NJ in his crib and ran to her husband's bedside.

"Baby, what *is* it?"

"I don't know! All I know is that I can't live like this! I've tried! The therapy ain't working! My son wants me, I can't hold him! I can't hold you! What am I supposed to do? What kind of father am I?"

Tears began to flow, then he began to sob hysterically.

"You deserve *better*, baby!"

"Nigel, pull yourself together! We are not giving up!" Monica yelled, staring into his eyes, as she held his chin in her hands.

"Baby, just shoot me! Do it! Go get my gun out of the top of the closet and shoot me!"

"Satan, *you are a liar*!" Monica yelled, moving quickly towards the bedroom closet. She had no intention of getting the gun, but she was definitely grabbing a weapon! She came back with a little valve of holy oil. Nigel's dad had given it to her at the hospital. She anointed herself, rebuking Satan. While speaking in tongues and crying, she went back into the other room. She proceeded to anoint her baby then she went back to Nigel. She anointed his head, temples, and arms as he laid there crying. Monica grabbed the draw sheet on the bed and quickly rolled him over in one quick, swift move. She used to be a CNA and now her skills were coming back. In the Holy Ghost, she anointed Nigel's spine and his back.

As she rolled him back over, he continued to speak foolishness and Monica continued to pray.

"I wish he would've killed me! I can't walk! I'm a nobody! He should've just taken me out! Can you imagine what it's like for me, to lay here listening to you and the little guy go on, without me! You have no more use for me. Heck, I need you!

I'm tired of you doing everything! You have to feed NJ, then feed me! Bathe NJ, then bathe me! Change NJ, then change me! Put the oil down, Monica! Come on and do us all a favor!"

Monica couldn't believe the words that were coming out of his mouth! Obviously, he was slipping into a rage. Monica didn't know what to do. She'd never seen him like this before.

Quickly, she ran into the room and grabbed her cell phone. Bryan picked up on the third ring.

"Bryan," she sobbed.

"Monica, what's wrong?"

"Bryan, I don't know! I don't know what to do! He's gone mad! He's crying and speaking out of his mind! Bryan, he wants me to take his gun and kill him! I think he's having a nervous breakdown!"

"Lord have mercy! Hold on Mon, I'm on my way!"

Bam, bam, bam! Bryan banged on the front door.

"Monica! Monica girl, who is that? Did you call somebody? Who did you call? Did you call my mama?

Please tell me you didn't wake up my mama!" Nigel yelled from his bed.

Monica ran towards the door, struggling to tie her housecoat. Bryan lived about eight minutes away, but it seemed like he arrived in three. She opened the door to find Bryan there barefoot, in his long t-shirt and his boxers, stepping into his jogging pants as he waited for her to open the door.

"Sorry sis," he said as he pulled them up.

"Don't worry about it. Come on in, careful—don't wake the neighbors."

"Monica!" Nigel yelled from the bedroom.

"I'm here! Here I am. I'm coming, baby, calm down! You're going to make yourself sick and your blood pressure will go up."

"I don't care! he yelled.

"Hey, hey, man what's going on? asked Bryan, announcing himself as he walked into the bedroom.

"You called him instead of my parents? You called him?"

"Honey, I didn't want to wake them, I didn't know what else to do!"

"Come on bro, this is *me*, stop acting like I'm a stranger!"

"I know, I know … I just don't want you to *see* me like this," said Nigel.

"Like what?" Bryan asked.

"Broken! I'm *broken*, Bryan!" Nigel continued to cry.

"Okay, well first thing I think you need to do is, pull yourself together," Bryan began. What's this I heard about you wanting Monica to shoot you? Are you crazy? How could you even ask her to do such a thing? You know how much this woman loves you?"

"I know man, I'm just tired! Just ... just tired!" Nigel was sobbing again. "My wife and I have separate rooms. I miss my wife! I miss sleeping with her! Here I am stuck, I'm just stuck, Bryan! Helpless and hopeless," he cried.

"Okay, we can fix that. Monica, prep the bed."

At his command she ran into the other bedroom, grabbed some extra sheets, shuck pads and prepped his side of the bed. As she was doing so, the arm rail on the bed quickly went down.

"Bryan...Bryan, wait! What?"

Without saying a word, Bryan snatched back the cover and proceeded to pick him up.

"Hey man, what are you doing?" Nigel questioned, startled.

"I'm putting you in the bed with your wife."

"I didn't ask you to do that!"

"I know, but you just said that was what you wanted. Now come on!"

Bryan placed his arms carefully underneath Nigel's body and picked him up.

"Hey, Bryan, I think I'm good, I changed my mind ..."

"Nope! It's too late, it's 3:30 in the morning! I just came off a twelve-hour shift an hour ago,

Monica's going crazy because you're acting up, no sir...you will sleep with your wife tonight!"

Continuing to reach underneath again, he was stopped again.

"Hey, Bryan, wait...you know that I don't have any drawers on, right?"

"Well, I guess it's good that I'm not interested in seeing your little narrow behind!" he replied.

When Bryan lifted him into his arms, Nigel almost slipped out of them!

"Monica, *why* is he so greasy?" asked Bryan, preparing to carry him into the room.

"Never mind, come on," he ordered as Monica led the way.

"Catheter!" yelled Nigel.

"Got it," said Monica immediately, grabbing the bag from the side of the bed.

Bryan placed Nigel in the bed and Monica secured the bag with a long piece of velcro.

"Sis, can I get a pillow? I'm gonna hit the floor for a while."

"Yeah, sure thing. Please sleep on the couch." She handed him a blanket and a pillow.

"Nigel, are you good, are you okay?" asked Bryan.

"Yep," he replied.

Monica smiled and nodded at Bryan.

She walked over to Nigel with his cup that she retrieved from his room.

"Thirsty?" she asked.

Surely after all that he'd been through, he had to be parched! She turned out the lights and crawled into the bed beside him. "How does it feel to be in your bed?"

"Well, good, I guess... it definitely feels good being in this bedroom," he replied.

She just smiled and left him alone. She wasn't sure if he was rethinking the whole ordeal that had just happened. How could he ask her to do such a horrific thing? Maybe he was embarrassed because his best friend saw and had his hand under his naked behind. She didn't know. All she knew was that she was exhausted!

As she said her prayers, she asked God to please give them peace.

The next morning, she went into the living room, only to find that Bryan had let himself out and locked the door.

I guess he didn't want to wake me, she thought to herself.

As she went back into the room, she was stopped by the scene before her. Regardless of his condition, it was so good to see and feel her husband back in their bed again. She thanked God. Her thoughts were suddenly interrupted by his snoring. Normally it was aggravating, but this time it was like music to her ears. It brought a smile to her face.

Well mister, after last night you should *be tired*, she thought as she leaned over the bed and gave him a kiss on the forehead, then checked on NJ.

He was in his crib, in the corner, fast asleep. I can't believe you slept through all that, she thought, covering him up again. The poor child hated being under the covers.

Finally, she returned to bed.

Later that day, there was a knock at the door. It was Bryan.

"Hey sis, I'm on the beat. Just checking to see if everything's still okay. Is he up?"

"I don't know," Monica replied.

"Yeah," called a voice from the bedroom. Monica and Bryan looked at each other and smiled. Monica chose to let them have their moment.

"So, how did you sleep last night, or shall I say this morning?

Did you get a little rest?"

"Yeah man, I slept like a baby. Being in my own bed with my wife knocked me out! It finally feels like I'm home."

"I bet! Well, I'm on the beat. I will be back by later tonight."

"Cool. See you then, stay safe. Oh, and Bryan? What happens in Vegas stays in Vegas."

"All day, every day!" he replied, smiling.

Nigel smiled back! "Thanks, bro."

"Anytime!"

"Bryan, you are *such* a good friend", Monica said, with tears in her eyes. "We thank God for you! I didn't know what else to do! I couldn't call his dad. He's elderly and really doesn't need this kind of drama in his life! He loves that boy so much! I know he'd have a heart attack at the mere thought of Nigel being suicidal! I'm sure that his heart couldn't take it!"

"It's okay Mon, you did the right thing. Now dry those tears, I will see you guys tonight."

"Bryan, God has an awesome wife for you. I'm praying for you."

"Amen, I agree, sis! Now, kiss my godson for me."

CHAPTER FIVE

All day there was an elephant in the room. As painful as it would be, the issue had to be addressed. Monica just wasn't sure how to approach it! It was apparent that Nigel was embarrassed. She only hoped that he would be the one to bring it up. She was so grateful that this little incident happened on the weekend. She couldn't ask for more time off even if she wanted to. She spent the morning in the den working on a special project. Nigel's nurse and assistant came out to evaluate his progress and to get him out of the bed. Monica called them before they arrived and informed them of the breakdown and thus the new sleeping arrangement. Not knowing his mental status, they decided to totally ignore the fact that he wasn't in the hospital bed.

After they left, she presented Nigel with the gift. She figured it would be a good way of breaking the ice and talking about what happened last night.

She entered the room with a bag in her hand and NJ in the other arm.

"I know you heard me in there sewing all morning," she said, breaking Nigel's concentration on the TV. "I made you a present."

"Really? Why?" After last night's episode, he knew that a gift was the last thing that he deserved.

"Here, can you hold NJ for a second?" she asked.

"What? Monica, you know that I can't hold him," Nigel said sadly.

"Really? Then it seems like we need to fix that situation."

Monica walked over to the bed and laid the baby down. Then she took her special project out of the bag.

"What's that?" he asked.

When she turned around, she was holding an oversized baby apron. The straps were so long, they dragged on the floor.

"Okay now, let's try this again," Monica suggested. "Nigel, I need you to hold your son for a little while."

"Sure, babe," he replied.

Monica walked over to him, placed the baby apron on his chest, then the straps went over Nigel's shoulders, meeting side straps that were attached to in the back.

"Yep, I don't think that he's going anywhere," laughed Nigel.

Lastly, she put the baby in the oversized contraption and strapped him in. An overwhelming smile came upon his face, as he held his head down and felt the top of his son's head with his chin. He sat there for a while with his eyes closed, praying and enjoying the baby's aroma.

"So do you like it?"

"*Like* it, I *love* it! I love you, Monica! I don't deserve it. Monica, you never cease to amaze me. I'm sorry about last night! I truly am. I was crazy! Now here you are today, making another one of my dreams come true. I honestly don't deserve you."

"Well baby, we don't deserve God's grace either, but He still gives it to us. As a matter of fact, He gives us a new dose of mercy every morning. Thank you, Jesus, because by 11:30 p.m. most of us are riding on empty."

"Some people are riding on fumes," laughed Nigel.

That was one of the things that they had in common. They both liked to have fun and laugh. Nothing like good humor to settle an argument.

"Thanks babe, you don't know how much this means to me. I'm in a tough situation here. I know you are doing everything possible to make it better. Please forgive me in my irrational moments. I don't mean to add to the burden."

"Nigel, I have all confidence that we will get through this. Now, be quiet before you wake your son. Maybe tomorrow I'll figure out a way for you to change him. As for now, I'm

going to start dinner and do some laundry."

"Yes, ma'am," Nigel replied.

She blew him a quick kiss, then quickly turned and sashayed out.

"You know that you're wrong for doing that, right? So wrong," he laughed.

"I gotta keep your mind strong!" she yelled as she went towards the kitchen.

"Yeah right," said Nigel.

Nigel had been home for nine weeks. The doctor was right. With the help of his therapists, the progression was better since he returned home. At this point, he was able to move his arms a little and squeeze a tennis ball.

The home health assistance was a lifesaver for Monica. Ciara sat with Nigel every day while Monica worked.

One day Monica got caught in a last-minute meeting which turned into a business dinner. Monica kept glancing at her watch. She knew it would soon be time for Ciara to leave. When the meeting was adjourned, she left and raced home. She pulled up into the yard to find Ciara's car still in the driveway.

Monica usually announced herself when she entered her home, but this time she didn't. She already felt bad about keeping Ciara waiting. She opened the front door to find NJ fast asleep on the living room couch. Bryan must have picked him up from the daycare, she thought.

Next, she peeped into her bedroom only to find it empty. However, the door to Nigel's bedroom was partially cracked. Monica was not mentally prepared for what she was about to witness.

She pushed the door open only to find Nigel in the hospital bed with only a towel over his lap. Ciara stood at his bedside with his bath water and a nice lather of soap on Nigel's chest!

"Young lady, please tell me *why* you are bathing my husband!" yelled Monica as she yanked the door open.

"Oh, ma'am, I was just…"

"Leaving," Monica interrupted. "But before you go, do me a favor and pull out your duties list from the company," she said sternly, only making eye contact with Nigel.

Ciara did as she was told.

"Read them to me!" Monica ordered.

Ciara read her the duties.

Now, do you recall reading anything stating that you are to *bathe* my husband?"

"No ma'am, I was just trying to do you a favor and…"

Once again Monica interrupted. "Sweetheart, when I need a favor, I'll ask you for one.

Which will never happen, because you're being dismissed! I will no longer be needing your services!"

"Monica!" Nigel yelled. "Monica, baby she was just trying to help out while waiting on you."

Monica quickly gave Nigel the "shut up" look and he got her loud and clear! He knew by the look in her eyes that she was about to explode.

"I don't want to get fired," Ciara pleaded as she walked out the door. "Ma'am, I just…" This time, her thought was interrupted by the slamming of the door. Monica stormed back into the room and stood there facing Nigel, her hands on her hips.

"I really *don't* believe what I just saw!"

"Babe, she was just trying to help."

"Nigel, this isn't about her—it's about *you*! You know that I'm the only person that bathes you. It's been that way since you got in this condition! Is this your way of cheating on me? You'd better tell me something, Nigel, and it better be good!"

"Monica, what? Cheat on you? In this condition? Woman, have you taken a good look at me lately? I never cheated on you when I had legs that worked!"

Without saying a word Monica grabbed her baby's bag, her purse, NJ and the keys. She walked out and slammed the door.

"Monica!" yelled Nigel.

He heard as her car started. *I know this girl is not leaving me here like this alone*, he thought. His heart dropped as he heard the car spin out of the yard. There he was, lying helplessly, with only a towel across his lap and the sheet gathered at his ankles.

Reality quickly set in. *Oh my God! What have I done?* He thought.

Monica cried as she drove to Nigel's mom's house. No matter how mad she was, Monica wasn't heartless. She picked up her cell and hit the speed dial.

"Hey sis, what's up? asked Bryan.

"You might want to go by the house. I'm gone for the night and I'm sure your brother is going to need you."

"What do you mean you're gone? You left him there alone?"

"Yep!"

"My God, Monica, what's going on?"

"I'll be back tomorrow, maybe…"

Once again Bryan flew to his partner's rescue.

He rushed into the house to find Nigel in the bed, half naked with his bath water on the stand beside him.

"Man, what in the world is going on?" asked Bryan, covering Nigel with the sheet.

"Bro, I screwed up! The only thing I had left, just left me."

Fighting back the tears, Nigel began to explain.

"I was just trying to help! The therapy has me where I can work out my hands but I can't lift my arm over my head yet. What harm could have been done?"

"So this was *your* idea! Dude, I'm not telling you to lie to your wife, but do not voluntarily give that information. It would devastate her! Look at it from her perspective. We all know that you have always been a chick magnet. Even on the beat, you have to fight off the ladies.

"Yes, you're paralyzed, but there is nothing wrong with your mind. Here, your wife—your faithful wife, the one that does everything for you and never complains—walks in and finds a pretty, younger woman rubbing on her handsome husband's chest, giving him a bath! Doing *her* job! You know how territorial Monica can be. She barely asks your mom for help. In her eyes, you are *her* job, her problem."

"Jesus, I'm stupid! But that's my point exactly; she's tired, Bryan. I know it. I can see it in her eyes."

"Honestly, the situation doesn't look good no matter how you slice it. You crossed the line, Nigel."

"Can you call her, please?

"Are you sure that you want to do that?"

"Yes! We never go to bed angry."

Bryan dialed Monica's cell and the call went to voicemail.

"Use my phone and call her mother, please," suggested Nigel.

Bryan did so and put the phone on speaker. Nigel was embarrassed and even more stressed when his mother-in-law informed him that his family wasn't there. He had to explain what happened, and now his mother-in-law was upset.

A few minutes later, Nigel's dad called. Bryan put him on speakerphone. Nigel knew by the way that he said his name that Monica was there, spilling the beans.

"Son, I will be over to sit and talk with you tomorrow evening."

"Dad, can I speak to Monica?"

"Nope, let her breathe for tonight, son, talk it out with her tomorrow. She's not ready yet."

"Yes, sir." Nigel hung up the call.

"For the love of God! I expected her to go to her mom; but she had to take it to the preacher! Now I'm looking like an idiot before the whole family!"

"Chill out bro, it'll blow over!" Bryan reassured him. "Until then, I've ordered a pizza for us. We can watch a movie and make the best of it."

Bryan had never been a caregiver before. He'd forgotten the fact he'd have to feed Nigel, brush his teeth, rotate him and pray with him before bed.

It was in that moment that he got a small sense of why Monica felt betrayed. He could only hope everything went well through the night. Nigel was truly his best friend, but he'd just about had enough of his nakedness.

Just as predicted, at the crack of dawn the front door inched open. Monica was slipping back into the house. She went into her room and closed the door. Bryan and Nigel both heard her, but dared not say a word.

"She's back," Nigel whispered.

"Yep, told you," Bryan whispered back from his pallet in the corner.

There was a lot of commotion going on in the bedroom. Surely wasn't going to work this morning.

"I guess she's getting ready for work," mused Bryan.

"Who's going to stay with me?" Nigel wondered aloud.

"Not me," said Bryan quickly. "I'm out!" They both laughed.

Just as Bryan turned on the light to find his shoes, the door popped open.

"Bryan, can I speak with you?" Monica asked.

"Don't you want to come in here?" said Bryan nervously, as Nigel eyed them both.

"Nope, it will only take a second, Bryan."

"Are you sure it's safe?"

"Yes, I'm completely dressed. I don't lay around half-naked," Monica said wryly.

Nigel could only close his eyes against this low blow!

"Okay, give me a second. What should I *do*?" he asked Nigel, trying not to be disrespectful to his friend.

"Go," Nigel whispered.

At that moment Nigel had an epiphany. He felt sick to his stomach! Although he trusted Bryan, it made him desperate to think of another man in the bedroom alone with his wife. He could only imagine how Monica felt.

Bryan stood in front of the open door, refusing to go into the bedroom.

"What's up, sis?

"First, I want to thank you for last night. I might have overreacted a little bit, but Nigel knows how I am."

"Yes, he does," agreed Bryan.

"Throw me under the bus, why don't you?" mumbled Nigel, lying in the bed straining to listen.

"God-daddy, I know it's your day off, but can I dare ask you for one more favor? Can you take NJ to Lisa's sister's house for me? It's out of my way and will make me late. Mom called and said that she's babysitting my sister's kids, who have chicken pox."

"Yeah, sure. Give me the address."

"Who's going to stay with me?" Nigel yelled out from the other room, now concerned.

"Your mama!" Monica yelled back, as she handed Bryan the baby.

Bryan tried desperately not to smile.

Monica then stormed into Nigel's room to finish the confrontation.

"Since you want to be bathed by a woman other than your wife, I figured it might as well be the one that gave birth to you! Today, your mama will be sitting with you and she will be bathing you!"

Nigel was speechless!

Monica put his medication on the nightstand. Suddenly, the doorbell rang.

"That must be her, now."

"I'll let her in," volunteered Bryan, still trying not to smile.

"Come on, Monica—I'm sorry, baby, don't do this. My mom, really? I know that I hurt you. I didn't mean to and I said I'm sorry. Seriously, babe, stop! Monica, Monica, please!" Nigel pleaded.

Without thinking, Nigel leaned over and grabbed Monica's arm, almost falling out of the bed!

"*Nigel!*" she yelled.

His mom and Bryan rushed to the door to see what was happening. She couldn't believe it. No, actually she *could*; she knew that God would answer her prayers! Thus, the lovers' quarrel was over!

Monica planted kisses on his face, then sat on the bed, leaned over into his chest and cried!

Nigel felt awful.

"Nigel, hold me. Do it, hold me! I need you to hold me, right now!"

Without thinking, Nigel moved his other arm and pulled her into an embrace!

Monica began to sob. His mother fell onto her knees, praying and thanking God. Bryan eased out of the front door with the baby, wiping tears from his eyes.

"Looks like we'll have a reason to be calling the doctor," came his dad's voice from the bedroom door, where he'd just appeared. Monica was beyond happy, she was ecstatic! She knew that it would be difficult to focus at work, but unfortunately, she had to go. The doctor said that he'd stop by that afternoon, after Monica had returned from work. Until then, Nigel knew that he'd have to deal with his folks. His folks thought the world of their daughter-in-law. He knew that he was still in trouble.

It's amazing how that feeling never goes away, that level of fear, reverence and respect for your parents, no matter how old you are. Your parents are still your parents.

"As happy as I am for you, Nigel, we still must address the elephant in the room. I don't get it! I don't understand, son, what in the world were you thinking? God has blessed you with a jewel!"

"I know, Dad, I wasn't trying to be unfaithful or inconsiderate. I was only trying to help; but in hindsight, I now regret it all! I should have just waited for Monica."

"Well, I agree with Monica. That little floozy probably already had an eye for you. A few smiles and flirts to stroke your ego and then my poor son couldn't think straight. Trust me son, every smile ain't genuine!" said his dad.

"I don't even know how you face her," his mom put in.

"I can't. I've tried, but she won't forgive me. I almost fell out of the bed on my head trying! I can only continue to ask for forgiveness and pray that it is granted."

"Well, it looks like one good thing came out of this, son, you miraculously regained your upper movement. It was the light out of darkness. But now, I'm going to step out and let your mama give you a bath."

"Dad, please," pleaded Nigel.

"Oh no, you are swallowing this pill on your own. I'm not an ogre, I'll be back to take care of your manly areas."

"Thanks dad," replied Nigel.

Lord, you're really whipping me good on this one, he closed his eyes and laughed to himself. *I got it! Never take your "good thing" for granted. I hear you, Lord.*

CHAPTER SIX

D r. Allen kept his promise and stopped by once Monica had returned home.

"Well, it's good news. He's getting better, but not quite out of the woods yet. With the help from therapy and family, slowly but surely, I believe he'll get there."

Nigel's parents stayed to help him for a week. Finally, Monica decided she would allow home health assistance once again, but no more pretty young things. She agreed to Miss Maxine, age 67. Monica could tell by her profile that she was a pistol! She was ex-military and just what they needed. She treated Nigel like he was a soldier. Everything was by the book!

Bryan continued to drop the baby off at Lisa's sister's house every morning.

One day, Lisa called Monica on her lunch break.

"It seems as if Bryan and Leslie hit it off real well," Lisa began.

"What do you mean by 'hit it off'?" asked Monica.

"Girl, you know that I'm not the type to gossip, but my sister just left my house. She came over to find a dress. It seems as if she has a date with a 'Mr. Bryan'.

"What? Really? He hadn't mentioned anything to me about it. Oh Lisa, I think they would make a lovely couple. No *wonder* he's been eagerly dropping NJ off every morning!" They both laughed.

"Yes, my sister has been through a lot and she deserves a good man. I think she's finally over Pete's death and ready to move on."

"Well, she's found a winner in Bryan," said Monica. "He's one of a kind. Let's agree to stay out of it, pray and let God do the work!"

"Amen," said Lisa. "How's things coming along with Nigel?"

"His body is healing slowly, and he's regained some movement, thanks to the home therapy...Just keep us in prayer."

"I will, my sister."

"Oh my, Lisa, let me go. I feel like I'm going to be sick. I will talk to you later."

Monica threw her cell down and ran into the bathroom.

"What's wrong, Monica?" Amanda called out.

The office was so tiny, everyone could hear everything! It was obvious that she was throwing up! Amanda stood outside the door, waiting to help her when she came out.

"Hey love, are you okay?" Amanda asked, guiding Monica by the arm.

66

"I don't know, I felt bad yesterday and even worse today."

"Monica! Are you pregnant?" asked Jennifer.

"That's a silly question. My husband's paralyzed."

"Actually, some paralyzed men can still conceive children. Besides, your husband's injuries are not permanent, it could be possible."

"Also remember, he moved back into your bedroom," teased Jennifer, winking.

"When was your last period?" questioned Amanda.

"My period! Oh my God! I've been so stressed, I forgot about my period!" Monica ran to her desk and pulled out her pocket calendar. "It's been almost four months!"

"What? Four *months*, seriously? How could you possibly forget your period for four months?" cried Amanda.

"Guys, you don't understand. With everything that's been going on with Nigel, I have been living in survival mode! Honestly, I totally forgot about it. But, how *could* I forget my period? This means another baby—no, I *can't* be pregnant!"

"Well, there's only one way to find out. I'll be right back. I'm going to the store across the street," Jennifer volunteered. Within minutes she was back, with a pregnancy test in her hand.

"Here, girl, go ahead and make it official." She handed Monica the test. Monica went into the bathroom, peed on the stick and within minutes it was official. Monica was pregnant! Tears begin to roll down her face.

It was definitely accurate, the morning sickness verified it.

"What are you going to do?"

"What do you mean, what am I going to do? I'm going to tell my husband that we are having a baby. Oh Lord, just saying that makes my stomach queasy."

She folded her arms and laid her head down on her desk. Amanda gestured for Jennifer to go out and help Brandi with the customers. She then pulled up a chair and sat there quietly, rubbing Monica's back.

"I tell you what, dear, it's a slow day. People will only be coming in to pay premiums, because it's the end of the month. Why don't you go home and lay down? I'll cover for you."

"Thanks Mandy, I could use the time. I just need to get my thoughts together."

Monica left the office thinking about her current situation.

She wanted to pray and talk to God like she normally would do—only this time, she didn't know what to say. However, she knew the Holy Spirit did. She spoke in her Heavenly language all the way to her mom's house. She wasn't sure if her nephews still had chicken pox, so she sat in the driveway and called.

"Hey, ma…"

"What's wrong, Monica?"

"Ma, are the kids over the chicken pox?"

"I think so. They still have a few bumps, but I think they're fine."

"Can you come outside, please? I really need you to come sit in the car and talk to me."

Without a "yes" or even hanging up, Miss Rhonda was on her way! In seconds the passenger door opened and her mom got in the car.

"Baby, what's wrong? You're scaring me!"

"Mama, I'm pregnant!" Monica said, as tears rolled down her face.

"Is that what this is about? You had me thinking that the world was about to end!"

"Yes, that's it—and I'm scared! Mom, I have a 14-month-old baby, my husband is paralyzed, I'm the sole provider and now I'm pregnant! I feel like I'm in a storm!"

She continued to cry.

"Mama, what am I going to do?"

"Well, the first thing that you're going to do is dry those tears. Then you're going to thank God for your baby and stop treating it as if it were a curse. Only God can give life! Yes, this is going to be another thing on your plate. But the good thing about storms is that they don't always last. The sun will shine again."

Immediately, Monica sighed and laid hands on her belly.

"Mom, please pray." Her mom laid her hands on Monica's belly as well and began to pray.

"Dear heavenly Father, we thank you for your love and your wisdom; although we might not understand your timing, we know that your thoughts are not our thoughts and your ways are not our ways. We thank you for this little ray of sunshine that Monica is carrying. We know that children are a gift from you. Now we ask you to bless it and we pray for a healthy baby and safe delivery. Please strengthen my child, oh Lord. I know that she's stronger than she thinks—in Jesus' name, amen."

"Thanks, Mom. I always feel so much better when you pray."

"There's nothing like a mother's prayer," said her mom.

"Amen to that! It's an amazing feeling to know that your mom's always in your corner! It is so important to have a praying circle. For the moments when we can't pray for ourselves."

"That's so true, honey," Ms. Rhonda agreed.

"Well, I guess I'll go home and tell my husband. I don't know how he's going to react, but *we're having a baby!*"

Monica drove home, praying that Bryan was still there and that God would give her the words to say.

"Hey, dudes!"

She entered the apartment to find Nigel in the wheelchair and Bryan sitting on the couch, watching the basketball game.

"Monica, what's wrong?" said Nigel immediately.

He knew his wife. He could tell that she had been crying.

"Nothing," she said as she walked over to her husband and gave him a little kiss.

"Come on, Monica. When does 'nothing' leave tears in your eyes? I know when something is wrong!"

"Well, I won't say something is wrong, but I do have a little surprise for you, both of you actually.

"Nigel, give me your hand," she commanded.

Nigel extended his hand slowly. Monica opened her purse and placed the stick from the pregnancy test in his hand.

Nigel's eyes grew large as soon as he saw the stick.

"*What?*"

Slowly he brought it up to his face for a closer look.

"You're pregnant! This says that you're pregnant!" Nigel yelled, dropping the stick. "Did you just really put that pee-pee stick in my hand?"

"Yes, I did and yes it does! You are going to be a daddy, and you, Bryan, are about to be a God-daddy again!"

"Wait! Hold up! How did this happen?" asked Bryan, rubbing his head.

"Yo, bro … I think that's my line, but yeah, Monica—how in the world did that happen?"

"Calm down, the both of you. I've just been so stressed out lately that I hadn't noticed that I missed my period. Not until I started throwing up today."

"Throwing up? Baby, that means morning sickness! Which also means that you're a

few months' pregnant! How are you feeling?"

"I'm fine. Full of mixed emotions. I'm still trying to figure it out. I'm always tired. I thought that I was stress eating, but now I understand all of the extra food."

"Monica, you are definitely stressed out. I can tell that you are losing weight.

So you're telling me that he can still have children? *Wait* a minute, I hope that this wasn't the night that he was acting all crazy and had all of that oil on him? I had the joker in my arms! For Pete's sake!"

"No, that was *holy* oil, Bryan," clarified Monica.

"You know what, I think I'm going to leave you two to discuss this one. All I'm going to say is that I hope it's a girl! I will talk to you guys later. I need to go run some errands and maybe do some God-daddy window shopping."

"No shopping yet, Bryan!"

"Yes ma'am," he responded.

"Okay, but I'd be lying to say that I'm not excited as always! Don't worry, count on me! I'm going to be here for the both of you."

"Thanks, man," said Nigel appreciatively. "Wow, another baby … just the thought of it takes a moment to process."

"Don't worry, honey, everything will be fine," said Monica.

Over the next few days Nigel was very quiet. It was obvious that he was doing a lot of thinking. He also was becoming quite protective. He barely wanted her to do anything.

He was still slowly improving. It seemed as if being transferred out of the rehab facility was a blessing in disguise. Nigel was now able to feed himself, shave and no longer used his baby apron.

The news of Nigel's progress traveled quickly through the precinct. The Chief and the rest of the squad were elated to hear that Nigel was doing much better. An officer from the K-9 unit heard about Nigel and stopped by for a visit with the Chief. It seems as if they had an overflow of dogs. The younger dogs had graduated and would now be replacing the older ones. The dogs were well trained and animals were known to be very therapeutic.

They'd also been experimenting with different breeds. Now that the experiment was over, they were trying to find them good homes.

"I was thinking that a dog could aid Nigel's recovery," said the officer.

"Well, let me run the idea by his partner and his wife Monica first," suggested the Chief.

Bryan was having mixed emotions about the idea. Although he agreed in principle, he hated the thought of yet another thing going on Monica's plate. Surely Nigel wasn't able to take care of a dog. Adding a dog to the picture would be like adding yet another baby! Nigel met him on his arrival, with Monica in the kitchen cooking dinner while NJ and Nigel watched TV.

It warmed Bryan's heart to see Nigel open the door.

"Hey hey family, I come bearing good news! I have a proposal for you guys," he began.

"Well, on that note, come on into the kitchen," said Monica. "You can tell us all about it while we eat."

"Spill the beans! What's up?" asked Nigel.

"Well, one of the directors from the K-9 division came to visit the Chief today."

"Don't tell me that you are trading me for a K-9!" Nigel exclaimed.

"Never!" he quickly responded.

"You guys have seen those documentaries where handicapped individuals are assisted by a dog ..."

"A *dog*! No, Bryan!" It was Monica's turn to exclaim.

"I know, sis! They have an overflow of dogs right now. They're trying to find them good homes; Nigel was selected. Everyone knows his story and the word of his progress is getting around. They thought that it would be a major asset towards the final goal; him walking again. Not to mention, these dogs are getting old. It won't be easy finding them a home. If they are taken to the pound, there's a great possibility that they will be put to sleep."

"I don't know, Bryan," said Monica.

"Yeah, bro, as much as I want to say yes, even I can't ask it of her. My wife's plate is full!"

"I will help you. Nigel can too, now that he is able to use his hands."

"Yeah, but even with that, Bryan, I still would have to go with him. I can't have Nigel out on the streets in his condition by himself!"

Monica frowned.

She could tell by the look in Nigel's eyes that he really wanted the dog.

"How about we try it out for a week. If we find it to be too overwhelming, then we will give the dog back," she said.

"Sounds good to me. "What do you think, Nigel?"

"I agree, one week trial!"

"Awesome. I don't know when he will be ready. There's a process and the dog has to be cleared before they give him to you. However, we should get things in motion. Let me call the Chief."

"Go ahead. We're excited!" said Nigel.

"Yep, excited…" Monica mumbled.

"Hello Chief, just calling to tell you that Monica said yes—well, she didn't actually *say* yes. She actually agreed to the idea of giving the dog a one-week trial. Although she believes that the dog will be beneficial; she's afraid that the dog is going to be another overwhelming task. I promised to help her as much as possible."

"I will call the K-9 unit and get the paperwork rolling. The dog should be cleared in about two weeks," said the Chief.

"Well, just let me know when he's ready, and I will go pick him up."

Two weeks later Bryan received the call that Nigel's dog was being released. Bryan raced to the kennel, praying as he drove.

Lord, I know that you are in control, but I have a real good feeling about this. Work it out Lord! Amen.

The K-9 receptionist directed him where to find the dog and trainer. The large room was full of cages but very few dogs.

"Bryan?" she asked.

"Yes, ma'am," he responded.

"Good, I'm Destiny, one of the trainers. He's right this way."

Bryan admired her beauty as they walked towards the cage. For some reason, he was expecting a man. She was definitely not a man and it kind of caught him off guard. Actually, she made him a little nervous. His words were limited.

"You understand that the dog is not working, he's for therapy only...correct?"

"Yes ma'am, he will be only used for therapy. My partner is still in the wheelchair."

"We only have a few dogs left. We were informed of his condition and his family arrangements. Based on that, we decided that Winston would be most suited for him. Before I introduce you to Winston, I would like to explain that Winston was one of the dogs used in the experiment.

"We wanted to see what other breeds besides German Shepherds would be able to do the job efficiently. Surprisingly, Winston did a great job. I think he will be good for your friend."

When she opened the cage door, Bryan was surprised to see that Winston was a pug.

"He's a pug!"

"Yes, he is and he's a heck of a police dog."

"Wow, I would have never pictured a pug for a police dog," said Bryan, laughing.

"That's just it. Neither would the average gangster or dealer on the streets. In fact, most people don't know that they are hunting dogs, just with limited capabilities. However, this loveable bunch of fur has a heck of a nose. When trained correctly, they can be quite useful.

"How about you bring him over here? We have a few papers for you to sign, and he will be all yours."

As Bryan removed the dog from the cage, he realized that something was wrong with him.

"Wait! What's wrong with him?" he asked.

"He was run over while in the line of duty. It broke his hip and leg; unfortunately, it never healed properly. So he has a little limp."

"I see," Bryan replied.

Once the paperwork was signed, the pretty lady gave Bryan the dog along with a few toys and a leash. Within minutes Bryan and Winston were on their way. While Winston enjoyed the scenery from the window, again Bryan prayed.

Dear Lord, we thank you for this dog. I believe that he's perfect and a sign to Nigel. Let this dog give him the inspiration that he needs to continue to fight and recover. Amen!

Bryan stood in front of the apartment door with the dog on his leash. He took a deep breath and then knocked. Monica opened it, surprised to see Bryan standing there with Winston. She looked at the dog, then Bryan and gave him a thumbs up. Bryan took Winston into the bedroom. Nigel was sitting in his chair half asleep.

Bryan woke him by clearing his throat.

"Excuse me for interrupting your beauty nap, Officer Henderson, but I have a special delivery for you. I think you have a new friend who wants to meet you. Say hello to Winston, your new friend and assistance dog."

"Are you sure that you have the right dog? You guys gotta be kidding me! That's not a German shepherd, it's a pug! By the way, what's wrong with his leg? Is this what you think of me? OMG, they sent a crippled man a crippled dog?"

"Honey, you are sounding so ungrateful right now," said Monica.

"Well, I don't mean to. All I'm saying is, send a police officer a policeman's dog!"

"He *is* a policeman's dog, and from what I understand, one of the best. No he's not a German shepherd. He was actually an experiment. They wanted to see how well other breeds could measure up to doing the job. From what I was told, Winston did really well. That is until he was run over, while in the line of duty. He sustained a crushed pelvis and a broken leg that never healed properly. But it didn't stop him. Here he is ready for his next call of duty; to be your friend. All the old boy needs now is some tender and loving care."

Nigel continued to look at the dog with an expression of disgust.

"Well then, let's check him out, see what the old boy can do. There's a pamphlet in the box telling you his favorite treats and some commands," said Bryan.

"Look, Bryan, the dog is cute and I don't mean to seem ungrateful, but this is a joke! I can't, I won't accept this dog. I need a dog that can protect my family even if I can't!

Take him back! Tell the Chief and the guys to send me a policeman's dog!"

"Thanks Bryan, for everything as usual," said Monica.

"Yeah, thanks, Bryan. It's not that I don't like the dog. He just wasn't what I expected and definitely not what we need."

"Sure, but you know what's funny? God has a way of not always giving us what we want, but he always gives us what we need. Give the dog a chance, dude," pleaded Bryan.

"One week!" exclaimed Nigel.

"Deal. I'm going to head out now."

"No, Bryan, don't leave, stay for dinner. I'm making spaghetti."

"No thanks, sis, it's been a long day and I'm tired. I'll check on you guys tomorrow. I'll let myself out!"

"Nigel, how could you! That man bends over backwards to help you and your family. You could have at least *acted* appreciative!"

After a night of reflection and the silent treatment from Monica, Nigel woke up with a change of heart.

Bryan was right, this dog may be the blessing that he needed. He was ready to give the dog a chance and he wanted to show everyone by taking him on his first walk.

"Monica. Monica, are you awake?"

"Yes, Nigel," she replied dryly.

"Monica, you were right about my attitude yesterday and I'd like to say I'm sorry."

"Don't apologize to me, apologize to Bryan."

"I will. I will also give the dog a chance. I'd like to start by taking him for his first walk. Will you help me?"

After seven years of being married to this man, I still don't know why it's so hard to stay mad at him, thought Monica.

"Sure, we will make it a family outing," she agreed.

CHAPTER SEVEN

O nce she had everyone up and dressed, the Hendersons walked their new dog to the park. Nigel had NJ strapped in his lap and Winston's leash was tied to the powerchair, while Monica trailed behind. Her belly was getting bigger; with a baby on the way, she too needed the exercise. Later that day, Jeremy came over to give Nigel his therapy.

"Hey Jeremy, meet my new therapy dog Winston," said Nigel.

"Wow, I thought that the K-9 divisions mostly used German Shepherds?"

"Nope, not Winston. He's special!"

"I see," replied Jeremy.

"I would like to have a man-to-man talk," Nigel went on. "So, Jeremy, you know our situation. The wife is handling all of the responsibilities. She works, cooks, cleans, takes care of me, the dog, everything! Now that she's pregnant again she's always tired. I need to get out of this wheelchair, man!"

"What are you proposing?"

"I need you to come up with a plan that will get me back on my feet ASAP!"

"Now, you know that's impossible right? I mean, yes I can push you, but I can't make your body heal. What we definitely don't want to do is over-exert and do more harm than good. So for right now, I think that we should continue to take it slow, at least until I have a chance to discuss the matter with your doctor."

They agreed to continue the slow-paced therapy.

In the meantime, the pug seemed to be working out for the family. He was now the family dog. He loved NJ, obeyed commands and he was house trained. Bryan kept his word to come over and walk him frequently. One day just as Jeremy and Nigel returned from therapy, they met Bryan leaving the house. He waved as he backed out of the parking lot.

"I wonder where he's coming from?" Jeremy wondered.

"Probably walking the dog," Nigel replied.

Although he knew better, the scene looked somehow suspicious to him.

"Why was Bryan here?" He asked Monica as he rolled through the door.

"He came to drop off NJ's jacket. Leslie gave it to him last night, when they were out on another date. He also was planning on taking Winston for a walk. Since you weren't here, he said that he'd come back. He's going to pick up Leslie again today. I think they make such a good couple. I'm so hopeful for them."

"Your baby bump seems to be becoming quite large," said Jeremy, changing the subject.

"Yes it is! My body reminds me every day! I'm even beginning to waddle. I've been offered the chance to work from home. I think that I'm going to accept it. It would make my life a little bit easier."

Nigel and Jeremy's eyes met. Now he understood.

Monica's first day working at home turned out to be hectic. Nigel felt the need to roll out onto the porch, call Jeremy and vent.

"Hey man, I wanted to know if you had a chance to speak to my doctor about my therapy. Something has to change. I'm constantly praying for my wife, the baby...she's under so much stress right now. The phone keeps beeping with calls from people with insurance issues, the daycare is closed and NJ is teething and pooping.

Then there's me, the bills and the dog. I made a sandwich for myself today for the first time. I fed the dog too, all by myself. I'm trying, man, but it's not enough!"

"My friend, that's still great news. Therapy not only includes the physical, it also relies on the mind. The stronger the mind, the better. Now you continue to press and do the small things that you can to help her out. Not only will it help her, but it will also challenge you. You got this!"

Nigel's doctor did not approve the extra physical therapy. Instead, he ordered a couple of occupational therapy visits to enhance his motor skills. Before long he'd regained full function of his upper body. The timing couldn't have been more perfect.

Monica was beginning to have issues with the pregnancy. Her feet were swollen, she was experiencing chronic fatigue and dizzy spells. She worked as long as she could.

After a while, the task became too much for her.

Nigel talked Amanda into letting him take over Monica's calls and shift while she laid in bed and taught him the ropes.

Nigel was feeling like a man again. He was earning a living and taking care of his family. Bryan continued to help as much as possible.

It was now Christmas. Monica was on total bed rest and Nigel picked up a second job working for a travel agency. It was super busy! Their bedroom became the main attraction. It was where they worked, ate, played and spent quality time.

Life was hectic, but it was good. For the first time in a long time Nigel felt in control. One night, after a full day's work, Nigel ordered Chinese food. He fed his family, bathed NJ in the bathroom sink and prepared Monica and himself for bed.

"I'm worried about you," said Monica.

"I'm fine," Nigel said, as he eased out of his wheelchair and into the bed. He was so exhausted, it seemed as if he was asleep before his head hit the pillow.

During the night Nigel was frantically awakened by the sound of a loud boom and Winston's barking. Something definitely fell and it sounded like it came from the kitchen.

"Monica, babe, did you hear that?" Nigel whispered in the dark.

Unfortunately, there was no response.

"Monica! Monica," Nigel frantically felt the other side of the bed in the dark. The bed was empty. She wasn't there! Where was she?

"Monica! Monica!" Nigel yelled. He was greeted by silence.

Now panic began to set in! He threw back the covers and turned on the lamp.

Sure enough, she wasn't there!

Jesus!

He threw his legs over the side of the bed and pulled himself into his wheelchair. He had to find her! He flipped on his mobile chair, only to find out that it was dead!

Lord have mercy! I forgot to plug in the power cord!

"Monica!" He yelled again as he reached for his cell phone. He immediately called Bryan.

"Bryan, I need you!" He yelled hysterically without even saying hello.

"Nigel, what's wrong?"

"It's Monica! Man, I think she fell in the kitchen and I can't get to her. My power chair is dead! Can you come over quickly? She's not answering me!"

"Okay man, but it's going to take about 20 minutes—Leslie and I are in Charlotte! I'm on my way!"

"What's going on?" asked Leslie.

"Monica passed out and Nigel can't get to her. We need to go to them."

"Then let's go!" she replied.

Nigel quickly dialed 911.

"Yes. My name is Officer Nigel Henderson. My pregnant wife fell in the kitchen and I can't get to her because I'm paralyzed—please come quick!"

He then threw the bed pillows onto the floor and threw himself off the bed. Even the extra therapy didn't prepare him for the work out ahead. He dragged himself from the bedroom into the living room, screaming Monica's name. His arms were burning like they were on fire! It was dark and he couldn't see a thing. He stopped on the side of the couch and shined the flashlight from his phone into the kitchen. There she was, lying on the floor!

Nigel began to scream and cry! He pulled himself across the floor as fast as he could, but his legs were dead weight. He was a few feet away from her when he saw flashing lights.

"Help! Help me, please!" Nigel screamed.

The officers shined their flashlights into the window.

"Kick it! Kick it in now!" he yelled.

The officers did as he said, they kicked in the door and raced in!

It was two guys from his precinct.

"Thank you, thank you Jesus!" Nigel laid on the floor and cried.

They found Monica, passed out on the kitchen floor.

"Mrs. Henderson! Mrs. Henderson, can you hear me?"

"Guys please be careful, she's pregnant," Nigel begged through his tears.

Suddenly the paramedics rushed through the door.

"No, stop—take care of her! Don't worry about me!" he yelled.

With the lights on, Nigel could see Monica's motionless body lying on the floor. The sight of her helplessly lying there on the cold floor shattered his heart.

"Help me! Somebody help me get closer to her, please," he cried.

They ignored him and continued to work with her for a second trying to get a steady pulse.

"Family, we got one, but it's extremely low. We need to move now! Get Nigel up and let's go!" ordered the paramedic.

A few short seconds later, Bryan and Leslie rushed through the door. Nigel directed Leslie to get his manual wheelchair from the closet. He sat on the floor and cried silently as they put Monica on the stretcher and took her to the hospital. Bryan helped Nigel to slip on some jogging pants and they were off to the hospital as well. Nigel prayed and called on the name of Jesus over and over again. A lady officer stayed with Leslie and NJ until the house was locked and secured.

"I almost forgot to call our parents," said Nigel.

His hands were shaking so bad he could barely hold his phone. He called Monica's mom first. She picked up immediately.

"Nigel, what's wrong, is it time?"

"No ma'am, Monica fell in the kitchen. She's on the way to the hospital and her blood pressure is very low."

"What about the baby?"

"I don't know," he cried, "I'm not sure if she fell on it or not. We are on our way to Claymont University. It's closer."

"I'm on my way son, hold on!"

Then, he called his folks and gave the same information. Through the window, Nigel could see the paramedics constantly working with Monica. He anxiously watched all the way to the hospital.

"How is she?" he yelled as they pulled her out of the ambulance. Of course they couldn't tell him much. Monica's OBGYN Dr. Usher met them at the emergency room door.

"Dr. Usher, I don't know what happened," Nigel began, fighting back the tears.

"Do you know if she fell on her stomach or on her back?"

"No ma'am," when I found her, she was lying on her side in the middle of the kitchen floor."

"Dr. Usher rushed her up to the OB floor. She was there for a while being assessed and monitored. By now the whole family was praying and waiting.

"It seems like she'd tell us something," Bryan said. "I don't like to use my badge, but bro, just give me the word and I'll go back there …!"

Nigel nodded.

Finally, the doctor came out to speak to Nigel.

"Mr. Henderson—" she began.

"No, just say it. Tell the whole family," he pleaded.

"Well, thank the Lord, when she fell, she landed on her side. Mom and baby both are stable. We are still monitoring them."

There was an explosion of praise and adoration in the waiting room.

"Do you know what caused her to pass out?" Nigel's father asked.

"Yes, it seems as if her blood sugar dropped too low. I think she was trying to make it to the refrigerator."

"Can we go see her? Me and my mother-in-law?" Nigel enquired.

"Yes, follow me." Nigel and his mother-in-law followed as the rest of the family went home.

Bryan went home to NJ.

Nigel held Monica's hand as she slept.

My Lord, how quickly things can change. Now, here I am on the side of the bed holding your hand. I'm going to give you the same message: fight and hold on, mama...fight for me, this baby and NJ. We need you!

Just as she seemed to be resting the baby's monitor went off. Monica was awakened by the alarm, followed by sharp pains and shortness of breath. The nurses and Dr. Usher rushed into the room and rolled Nigel out of the way as quickly as possible. The doctor went over to the machine and took a look at the stats. "Prepare the OR right away," she ordered. "The baby is in distress! We have to deliver now! We need an emergency C-section."

Nigel was allowed to scrub in so that he could hold Monica's hand. The doctor and the team left a clear path for Nigel to roll in and sit at Monica's side. Soon they were announced to be parents of a bouncing baby boy.

"Monica, are you okay?" Nigel kept asking his wife.

It seems as if she was fading in and out of consciousness.

"She's okay. She may just be a little buzzed and extremely tired, but she's fine, trust me," said the nurse. He leaned in to have a little talk while they finished up her surgery.

"Monica, I love you, girl," he whispered in her ear. "You know that you're my rib, right? I think I knew it in kindergarten. It was the day that I took your milk money and you kicked me in the shin." He smiled, reminiscing. "We're going to be okay. I thank God all the time for you and NJ. Now here you are, giving me another little one. I feel so selfish. All you do is give, give, give. One day, my queen, I'll be able to show you just how much you mean to me."

She opened her eyes and whispered, "I'm only doing my job. The job that God gave me. You give me your seed, and I'll give you a child. You give me groceries and I'll give you a meal. When you're able to give me a credit card, I'll give you the bill," She was smiling now.

"Soon, baby, soon. No questions asked. Now you rest, you've done your job for today and I love you."

"Shh, be quiet. I'm tired," she whispered, still smiling.

CHAPTER EIGHT

There they were again. In the hospital, in another tough situation, yet they were always able to find humor and joy. As the nurse returned with the baby and laid him in Nigel's arms, Nigel began to cry. He was speechless. He could only think of her lying on the floor and thank God that she didn't hurt herself or this little one.

"Are you okay?" asked the nurse, kindly.

"Oh yes, ma'am… I'm fine. Actually, I'm *perfect*. Don't worry, I got him."

"Okay, just call if you need me," she responded.

When the nurse returned to check on Monica, she found Nigel still sitting in his wheelchair holding the sleeping baby.

"I can lay him down, if you'd like?"

"No thanks, he's fine."

"What's his name?"

"Sampson—well, I still have to run it by his mom, but I like it. Yes, it's different, unique. He's a handsome boy, I think it fits."

"I think so too," she agreed.

"Well, thanks for your vote, stick around just in case I need you," he laughed.

When Monica woke up and regained her energy, she too approved of the name Sampson.

Monica made a quick recovery. Nigel and Monica's mom were taking turns helping with the babies. Sometimes both of them were there at the same time and they were enforcing the six weeks rule!

Sampson gave Nigel a newfound inspiration and will to fight for his life even harder. He knew that healing is partially mind over matter. It was definitely time to get back to work. Plus, there was no way that he could stay in a two-bedroom apartment with three women for the full six weeks. It had been three weeks already, another three would surely kill him! It was time to call the Chief!

"Chief Myers here."

"What's up Chief? This is Nigel Henderson.

I'm not sure if you've heard, but I have regained my upper body movement and strength. I'm hoping that you might have a desk job available for me? I have two young sons looking up to me. I know that the good Lord has brought me a long way, but I need to get on my feet again. I'm thinking a change of atmosphere could probably help. I can answer phones, file, whatever you need me to do."

"Sure, Nigel. Come in on Tuesday and I will give you your new assignment!"

"So soon—thanks Chief! I'll be there!"

Once he hung up, Nigel hollered and clapped his hands with joy! Now, all he had to do was figure out how he would get there. Of course, Monica came running into the room to see what was wrong.

"Nigel, what's wrong?"

"Nothing, nothing's wrong! Something is right this time! Baby, you are looking at Officer Nigel Henderson, desk cop!"

"What?"

"Sweetheart, I just got my job back as a desk cop. I start on Tuesday!"

"Are you sure that you are ready?"

"Yes, baby. Now let's change and get dressed. I'm taking you out tonight."

"Seriously, Nigel?"

"Seriously. Trust me."

"I can't go anywhere. Those two will barely let me sit on the porch! I don't think that I can bear hearing the 'stay in the house six weeks' lecture again."

"Monica, please do as I asked, close the door and let's just get dressed. I will handle them."

"Yes sir, officer," she saluted.

Monica did as Nigel asked. She helped him with his bath, then showered and dressed herself and assisted him. They both wore jeans and a plaid shirt. They looked like high school loves again.

"Okay, grab us a light jacket, then come and sit in my lap," said Nigel.

"Baby, no—I might be too heavy."

94

"You won't, plus I won't feel a thing. You do want to get out of this house, don't you?"

Monica opened the bedroom door and sat in his lap as Nigel drove them through the apartment.

"Oh, so that's what you guys have been up to," said Nigel's mom, smirking. "You look nice, but where do you think that you are going?"

"Well, in honor of getting my job back as a desk cop, I decided to take my bride on a date."

"In what?" her mother asked.

"In my wheelchair, mom. I won't take her too far. She needs a little air. I promise not to keep her out long. I know all about the staying-in-the-house-for-six-weeks-after-having-a-baby-thing. She'll be fine."

"I promise to put on my jacket," Monica chimed in.

"Alright, but don't keep her out too long, Nigel, please."

"Yes ma'am, we will see you two ladies shortly."

His mom opened the door and they were off! With her arm around her husband's neck, Monica couldn't help but smile as Nigel powered them down the sidewalk.

"Nigel, I hope that you have fully charged this thing!" Monica yelled as they whizzed down the street.

A few cars began to blow their horns.

For a moment, Monica was slightly embarrassed. Then she thought about how God had brought her husband from lying numb on his back to driving a mobile wheelchair. Her heart became overwhelmed and she leaned in for a quick kiss!

"Alright, girl! You do know that I need to see in order to drive this thing? What are you trying to do; make me dump you on the sidewalk?"

She laughed and kissed him on the cheek.

"Nigel, where are you taking me?" she asked as cars whizzed by.

"Almost there, just hold on a little while longer."

"Wait … oh my God Nigel, I know that we are *not* trying to cross this busy intersection in a wheelchair …!"

"Indeed we are!" "Ok babe, jump off and quickly press the button", Nigel ordered.

When the light flashed "walk", Nigel pushed the lever full force! Cars blew their horns and guys even hung out their windows. They cheered him on by whistling, while yelling "Go ahead, you got that pretty girl, boy!"

Monica laughed and buried her face in his shoulder. Not because of embarrassment, but she couldn't believe that they were actually crossing a four-lane road. Nigel didn't say anything because he knew that she was scared. However, that moment gave him a new sense of honor. Although he was in a wheelchair, she still trusted him as her man to protect her. She still trusted him with her life!

As the mobile chair jolted up onto the sidewalk, Nigel's thoughts were captured for a second by a funny feeling. For a second, he was sure that he could feel the firmness of her buttocks on his leg. He quickly dismissed the thought when she reminded him that she'd just had a baby; so easy on the bumps. He asked her to remain as she was until he asked her to get up. The wheelchair finally came to a halt.

CHAPTER NINE

"Okay Mon, you can get up and open your eyes."

"Mr. Jon's! Nigel, we used to come here all the time in high school. I had actually forgotten about this place!"

"Yep, it's still here. After all of those years, they are still in business."

"Let's get our usual old spot in the back so I can plug up my wheelchair. This baby has to get us back home."

As they ate, laughed, and enjoyed their meal, time slipped away!

"Oh my God, Nigel! We left at seven, it's now ten-thirty. They're never going to let me out again until the six weeks are up!"

"Well, I suggest that you enjoy the fresh air on the way home," he teased.

Nigel loaded up his bride, powered her back across the highway and to their home. He stopped at the end of the ramp for a long, intimate kiss.

"Are you ready?" he asked.

"I guess so."

"I can't believe that we are two grown-ups, scared to go into our own house!"

"What's even funnier is the fact that we had to beg to get out," Monica added.

"Okay, let's go," said Nigel.

"Oh wait, wait a minute," she said.

"One last breath of freedom, fresh air, and a kiss!"

Just as he slowly powered over the bump at the end of the ramp, he felt the sensation again. He smiled.

Then he threw his head back and laughed.

"Come on, Nigel, what are you doing? The moms are waiting on us, it's chilly out here and you want to play with your wheelchair!"

"Nope hon, I really wasn't playing with the chair. What would you say if I told you that I could feel that! Actually, I've felt you sitting in my lap all night. You know what that means, right?"

"Yes, your lower extremities are waking up!" Monica threw her head back in a joyful laugh.

Suddenly, the door opened. "Well it's about time that you came home! Nigel, bring that girl inside, she doesn't need to be in the night air!" ordered his mom.

"Yes, ma'am," he responded.

"Well, it looks like we just went from being grown, back to ninth grade again," Monica whispered into his ear.

Once inside, they revealed their little date night journey.

"You did *what*? You went across the highway together in a wheelchair? I don't believe it! For Pete's sake, Nigel, this child just had a baby!" his mom yelled.

"This is why you have to constantly pray for your children, even when they are grown! You just never know what they may decide to do!" scolded her mother.

"Now this is really beginning to feel like ninth grade," mumbled Nigel.

Monica smiled.

Finally the six weeks were up, the moms decided to go home and Nigel and Monica returned to being grownups again.

"Maybe next time we should call our sisters over to help out," laughed Nigel.

"Wait, what do you mean, *next* time ...?" questioned Monica sarcastically.

On Monday night, Nigel received a text informing him that the force would be sending a handicapped van to pick up himself and two other wheelchair-bound employees for work. The next day, Monica woke up early. She made sure that Nigel's uniform was ironed and his lunch was packed. When the van arrived, he was waiting at the door.

"Are you sure that you have everything, honey? Don't forget to take your twelve o'clock meds. I'll just call and remind you…" said Monica.

"Babe, calm down, I'm going to be fine! It's not my first day of school—poor NJ," he laughed.

"I know, but this is really your first time in public without me since the accident. I'm a little nervous."

Nigel pulled her into his lap.

"We have made it through the hard part, this is the easy part. I never could have gotten through it without you. It's time to get our lives back. Don't worry, I'm only a phone call away. The boys will keep you busy until I get home."

"Definitely," she agreed.

She sat in his lap quietly hugging him until it was time for him to leave. When the van's horn blew, Nigel nearly threw her out of his lap!

"Dang, Nigel!" she exclaimed.

"Sorry babe, I don't want to make them wait. I can't be late on my first day back!"

Nigel gave her another peck on the cheek and just like that he was off, whizzing down the ramp.

Monica peered out of the window, thanking God as she tried to fight the bittersweet tears that were rolling down her face.

"Good morning, guys, and when did the force start doing this?" Nigel asked, entering the van.

"Shortly after you were stabbed, a lot of things changed for us ... thank you," replied his coworker.

Nigel enjoyed the view as they traveled to the precinct. So many memories of being on the beat with Bryan, came flooding back! Once they'd arrived, he sat quietly waiting for his turn as the driver unloaded the van. He couldn't wait to see the crew again. He rolled into a decorated precinct, full of balloons, welcome back signs and of course tons of black licorice! They stood and clapped as he rolled in the door. Nigel couldn't hold back his tears, neither could a few others.

"Well, before he turns us into a bunch of crybabies, everyone welcome Nigel back and then get to work. Get in here son!" said the Chief, laughing.

"So good to see you, we all prayed for this moment. Now with that being said ... the corner desk on the end of row two is yours. You have a mountain of stolen license plates to track."

"Yes sir, fine with me. I'll get on it!"

"Welcome back, son! Now get on those plates!"

"Yes, sir, immediately," he saluted, smiling.

Nigel barely slept the night before. He couldn't wait to take his things out of his backpack and set up his desk. Finally, he was home. The first thing he sat on his desk was a picture of him and Monica. Then a few photos of the kids. Officer Arlington came over as he was setting up.

"So, I hear congratulations are in order."

"Yep, bouncing baby boy named Sampson."

"Is that him?" he asked, staring at the picture.

"Yep, that's him," replied Nigel proudly.

"Hmm, he looks like Bryan, I mean with the smile, freckles and sandy brown, curly hair ... cute kid though!"

"Thanks," said Nigel slowly. He felt like someone had knocked the wind out of him! He stared at the picture in awe!

Like a flash Officer Proctor slammed Arlington into the wall. He didn't know what hit him! Nigel was shocked and now the whole precinct was in an uproar as other officers rushed to get Proctor off of him.

"You stupid rookie, you have no idea what this man has gone through to get here! How dare you insinuate such a stupid insult about his wife to his face. You don't even know Monica!"

"Let him go! Proctor, he ain't worth it," said Reynolds.

The Chief made it out of the office just in time to hear pieces of what happened. He too was furious! He could see the hurt, embarrassment and now confusion in Nigel's face.

"Arlington, I need you in the office *now*!" he barked.

"Sorry about that, Nigel, I heard him and lost it for a minute. We all admire and honor Monica for being by your side every step of the way. I couldn't let him insult her, you or even Bryan like that."

"No, thanks man, you did what I probably would have done if I had legs that moved. Thanks, Proctor."

The whole atmosphere of the precinct had shifted. They all were now worried about Nigel. It was apparent that what Arlington said had his wheels turning. Neither he nor Monica had sandy brown curly hair.

A few minutes later Arlington was closing out his computer. He'd been put on a two weeks' suspension. From the looks everyone was giving him, leaving was the smart thing for him to do. He just didn't make it out before seeing Bryan.

The Chief called him off the beat to talk to him and fill him in on what had inspired. Things were bound to be rocky between him and his best friend.

Bryan gave Arlington a hostile stare as he walked into the Chief's office.

"He said *what*?" Bryan quickly snatched the office door open, but Arlington had slipped out.

"Nigel!"

His facial expression broke Bryan's heart. He ran to him.

"Nigel, brother… I hope that you know better. I love you bro, I would never do such a thing."

"I know, Bryan, man, it's cool."

His words didn't sound too convincing.

"Come on, the Chief told me to take you home."

"No, I'm fine. I can finish my shift."

"We know, I think he doesn't want you to overdo it on the first day."

"I didn't even get started!"

"It's okay. Go home, get some rest and start anew tomorrow."

"Yeah, I guess you're right."

The trip home was not the usual. The tension in the air was suffocating! Bryan kept thinking of something to say to break the ice, but his mind was blank. As he pulled into the driveway he finally spoke.

"Well, I know this isn't how any of us pictured your first day back would go, but we are grateful to have you back with us. Now, let's go in and update Monica."

Monica heard the van as it pulled into the yard. He was home early, too early! He had to be hurt! Putting Sampson his crib and NJ in his playpen, she marched out to see what was wrong. She arrived just as Bryan had lowered the lift.

"Hey guys, you are back early!" Bryan gave her a blank look.

"Oh my, Nigel are you—?" She didn't need to finish her thought, she could tell by his face that he was not okay. She looked at Bryan and he shook his head.

"I think we should go inside and talk for a while," said Bryan.

"No, it's okay, we don't need to."

"Nigel, yes we do! You guys are my family and this is my and Monica's reputation we are talking about here! Come on sis, we need to have a family meeting."

"What happened?" Monica questioned.

Nothing was said, both guys just proceeded into the house.

"Well, at work today…" Bryan started to explain, but Nigel interrupted.

"I'll tell her. She's MY wife," he blurted.

"Yes, she is. By all means, go ahead," Bryan agreed.

"Well, as you know, babe, I was put on plates duty. My job is to search for information on stolen license plates. I was at my desk, minding my business, when Arlington passed by, saying he'd heard that we'd just had a baby boy. I said yes and showed him Sampson's picture on my desk. He said, cute kid—he looks like Bryan!"

"What? He said what? What was he trying to insinuate?" Monica asked.

"I don't know! All I know is before I could blink, Proctor had him against the wall trying to choke the life out of him!"

"He was defending your honor, is what he was doing," Bryan added.

"The same thing that I would have done if I had been there. Needless to say, Arlington is on a two-week suspension. Orders from the Chief."

"Okay, so, Nigel, is this what this tension between you two is about? Nigel honey, you CAN'T be entertaining that thought! Are you questioning me as a woman? My loyalty? Bryan's loyalty? Our family love, your brotherhood?"

"No, no, babe, I know better," he replied, pushing the power button and rolling away.

Bryan gave Monica the under-eyed look.

"The Chief picked up on it first. His whole demeanor changed. That's why we are home early."

Monica quickly followed Nigel into the bedroom and knelt in front of his wheelchair. He sat quietly, peering into the crib as Sampson slept peacefully. Bryan followed.

"He does look like Bryan," Nigel whispered.

"*Nigel*!" She yelled.

"No way. Come on, man," said Bryan.

"Oh, so you believe him," Monica fumed. "I'm the woman that has done everything for you! I fed you, bathed you, clothed you! How could I have possibly had time to take care of Bryan's needs when I was so busy taking care of yours?"

She stood, quickly grabbed her frightened baby and ran into the dining room. Bryan found her sitting at the table staring into Sampson's cute little face. Tears were silently streaming down her face and lapping under her chin.

"I'm sorry, Bryan. I apologize for my husband. You have been more than a loyal friend. I just don't understand. Is this what he thinks of me? Why didn't he, my husband, verbally defend me?" she cried.

"I'm sorry sis, I think Nigel was just thrown for a loop. I'm sure that he didn't mean to hurt you."

The next few days were very awkward. Nigel wasn't himself. One evening as Monica was cooking her phone vibrated. She received a text from Bryan. Nigel leaned over for a clearer view. It said *meet me tomorrow, 10am at 409 West Parker Ave.* Nigel was furious but he didn't say a word. Now even he was questioning the character not only of his best friend, but his wife as well. He knew that Monica was trustworthy! However in the back of his mind, he was wondering what in the heck was going on.

Four days went by. Monica hadn't mentioned her private meeting with Bryan. It made Nigel even more depressed. It wasn't the type of depression that wouldn't let him get him out of bed; he just stayed standoffish, into himself.

Around 10 a.m. the following Monday morning the precinct was surprised by a special visitor.

"Monica?" said Nigel quizzically as he looked up from his desk to see his wife marching into the precinct with a yellow envelope in her hand. The fellows were happy to see her. However, one thing any man can recognize is a mad woman! They chose to stay out of her way! She stormed over to Nigel's desk and threw her phone before him, then she opened up the text that Bryan had sent her.

"Baby, what's going on, why are you here?"

"I'm here to prove a point, now Google it! Google the address that Bryan sent me. I know you read it because I saw you looking at my phone!"

Nigel did as he was told. He didn't want to be embarrassed more than he already was.

"What does it say? No, Nigel, read it out loud! What does it say?" Monica demanded.

"It says, Peter Saville Health Department."

"Thank you," she replied.

Monica quickly spun around and threw the yellow envelope on to Arlington's desk and placed her hand on her hip.

"Open it and read it, please."

"Me? What—why?" asked Arlington, mystified.

"From what I understand, you are the news anchorman of the precinct. Don't quit your job now!"

Arlington sat there like a deer in headlights. He didn't know what to do.

"Read the doggone thing! Do as the lady asked," Bryan yelled from the Chief's office door. Arlington picked up the yellow envelope, opened it and proceeded to read. "This I hereby declare by, the state of Georgia, is the results of the paternity records of Nigel Henderson, Monica Henderson versus Bryan Grey. I am hereby pronouncing that the results are conclusive, that Bryan Grey IS NOT the father of Sampson Henderson nor, Nigel Henderson, Jr. DNA results show that Nigel Henderson is 9 9 9 9 9 9 .99% the father of 5-month-old Sampson Henderson and 19-month-old Nigel Henderson, Jr. The records are conclusive, that Nigel Henderson is their father.

The whole precinct roared; they clapped so loud. Tears rolled down Nigel's face as he threw his hands up in surrender!

"Thank you to the Lord," he said.

When he opened his eyes, Monica was still standing there with her hands on her hips. Bryan was still standing in the doorway of the Chief's office with tears welling in his eyes.

"Monica, Monica baby—you didn't have to do this. I didn't ask you to do this!"

"I know you didn't! It was Bryan's idea. He was the one who wanted closure. Your loyal friend, partner and brother wanted to clear his name and my virtue once and for all!"

"Bryan, I'm so sorry."

Bryan couldn't respond. He didn't need to. The blank, disconnected look on his face said everything that he was feeling.

Nigel, on the other hand, was experiencing an array of emotions. He was happy yet sad at the same time. He was relieved to know for sure that Sampson was his child, at the same time realizing the price of the confirmation: it almost cost him his wife and his best friend.

"This is why it is so important to monitor who speaks into your ear. Some people are very good at sowing seeds of discord. Words are seeds," warned Chief Myers.

Nigel quickly grabbed the paternity results from the desk and rolled to the shredder. When they were done shredding, he took his left foot and placed it onto the floor, then the right one.

"Nigel ... what are you doing?" gasped Monica.

Without a word being said Nigel stood up from his wheelchair, and slowly took steps towards the Chief's door where Bryan was standing. Once again the precinct went wild!

His steps were slow, but they were steady!

He stopped to hug his wife. Bryan was headed towards them, but Nigel stopped him!

"No, Bryan, stay…this time, brother, *I'm* coming to *you*!"

On wobbly legs, step by step Nigel made it to his friend. Monica screamed and clapped in the background.

"Bryan, brother, I love you and I'm so sorry that I ever doubted you. I hope that you can find it in your heart to forgive me.

They hugged, then he reached into his pocket and pulled out a small envelope and handed it to the Chief.

"Seems like today is a day full of surprises." The Chief opened the envelope and read it.

"Nigel, are these your release papers? The doctor has cleared you to work?"

"Yes, sir, he has," he replied. Monica couldn't take it any longer. She ran into her husband's arms.

"Well then it's official, you're back! I guess this also means that you can have your old partner back," he said, looking at Bryan."

"Chief, mmm... I think I'm going to have to pass on that offer. I am totally fine with being a desk cop. I don't want to take any chances, because I have a loving wife, a best friend, and two young boys that need me!"

"Well spoken, from an honorable man. Now chop-chop, back to work! Never mind, I'm feeling gracious—take the rest of the day off and celebrate it with your wife. You'd better enjoy it, because next week, you will be working the entire week!"

"Yes, sir, Chief," said Nigel.

He gave him a salute and slowly walked back to his wheelchair. Monica followed him. Once he'd closed down his station, he packed his bag and gave it to Monica.

"Are you ready?"

"Yes," he replied.

"Well then, come on, hubby, let's go celebrate," she said, sashaying through the precinct with Nigel rolling behind her.

He could only shake his head and smile as the guys cheered. How quickly she'd forgotten that she was mad.

"Hey bro, Nigel...no!" yelled Bryan.

"Guys, come on, you know that's where babies come from right? We just had one!

Don't worry about it, bro, I got this," laughed Nigel as he exited the room, giving the deuces sign.

The precinct exploded with laughter and cheered!

CHAPTER TEN

It had been a long day. After Monica's surprise visit, paternity results, his walking revelation, then dinner and a movie, Nigel was exhausted! He and Monica showered together and went to bed. The next morning, he woke up still exhausted.

"Rough night, last night?" Monica asked.

"Yes, I kept having the same recurring dream, it freaked me out! I tossed and turned all night!"

"What was the dream about?" she asked.

"Believe it or not, I kept seeing the accident. I thought I was over it, but apparently, I'm not. It wasn't so much the accident that scared me, but the attacker. It was so vivid, he kept coming to me as if he were trying to tell me something."

"Wow, that is a little freaky," Monica agreed.

"Well, you rest, while I make us some breakfast. Then we will go to your parents and get the kids."

"Sounds like a plan," said Nigel contentedly.

After breakfast and a shower, Nigel and Monica went to the folks house to pick up their blessings. While the ladies prepared the kids to go home, Nigel and his dad spent a little quality time in his office.

As he rolled into the office and saw his dad sitting behind the desk, tears automatically began to flow!

His dad leapt to his feet and came to his side.

"What's the matter, son?

"Dad, something is going on. I don't know what's wrong with me. I keep dreaming about the guy that stabbed me, and just now I remembered lying flat on my back in the hospital, wondering if I'd ever see you preparing your Sunday sermons again.

By the Grace of God, Dad, I'm here with you!"

With a full heart, his dad held his hand as Nigel cried silent tears.

"Let it all out, son, God is good. As far as the young man goes, you know what to do. I also would like to see you and your family in church tomorrow."

"Yes, sir," he replied.

Yes, he knew what to do, pray for him. But there was part of him that didn't want to pray for him! Suddenly, the Holy Spirit reminded him how God gives us grace when we don't deserve it!

Nigel shared his father's request as they drove home. Sunday morning, Nigel and his family were in church early. They sat on the front row as the family always did. Nigel parked his chair in the corner. While his dad was preaching, he leaned over to Monica and whispered, "It feels so good to be back into the House of the Lord".

"Yes it does," she agreed, grabbing his hand. She could tell he was emotional.

When the sermon was almost over, his dad opened the doors of the church, asking if anyone wanted to give their life to Christ or rededicate their lives to the Lord. Without hesitation, Nigel stood up and slowly took a step. The church gasped in awe. His father

stood speechless as he clutched his Bible tightly to his chest, fighting tears. As Nigel slowly proceeded, his mom knelt crying and praying in the Holy Spirit. With tears streaming down, Nigel proceeded until he was standing before his father.

"Son," was all his dad could say, fighting back the tears as the church clapped.

Nigel took the microphone and began to speak. Monica rushed to his side, wiping his tears as he began to speak.

"I know that most of you know me and my story. I'm not a backslider, but with all that I've been through, I'd be lying if I said that there weren't moments when my faith wasn't weak. Moments when I couldn't pray for myself. That's why it's important to have a powerful praying circle of people in your life. I'm so grateful for mine. The Word says that, the effectual fervent prayer of the righteous man availeth much. I stand before you as proof. Is there anything too hard for God? No! God is still in the Miracle Working Business!"

His father anointed his head with oil. Nigel wept as he stood before his earthly father and heavenly father.

That night, Nigel dreamed about the prisoner again.

The next day, Nigel talked to the Chief about speaking to the prisoner.

"Do you think that's a good idea?" questioned the Chief.

"Yes sir, I do. I just want to talk to him. He keeps bombarding my dreams, night after night. I need closure."

"I'll get started pulling some strings now," said the Chief reluctantly

Around four the approval came through and Nigel was being escorted to see the prisoner. "Wait, not without me!" yelled Bryan as he raced behind them.

Nigel waited patiently behind the glass for the prisoner to come in. Bryan stood firmly against the wall behind him. When the prisoner entered the room and recognized Nigel as his visitor, he immediately began to cry and wail.

Both Nigel and Bryan were confused. His wailing was so heartfelt and intense, it moved Nigel. He forgot all about his need for closure, he wanted to know what was happening.

"Dude, thank you! Thank you for coming! I know that it was God!

I'm sorry, so sorry for everything!"

"Are you sure they got the right prisoner?" Bryan whispered.

The prisoner continued.

"I know that I did an evil thing to you. I found out that I'm in for life now."

"I would be lying to both of us if I said that I was sorry to hear that. You almost cost me my *life*, man! I was only doing my job!"

"I know, I'm sorry. Please forgive me," the prisoner pleaded.

"I have found the Lord and I'm a changed man, you gotta believe me. All I ask is for your forgiveness. I need it!

"Then you have it," said Nigel. "Yes, I do believe you. The Bible says, 'Therefore, if any man be in Christ, he is a new creature, old things are passed away, behold all things become new'. 2Corinthians 5:17. Honestly, I wasn't expecting the man that's before me. I forgive you and go in peace."

Without another word, Nigel signaled the guard, and they took the prisoner back to his cell.

"Thank you, I'm sorry for the pain that I caused you...Thank you so much!" he screamed as the guards escorted him away.

Nigel continued to nod his head, in forgiveness. For a moment, he sat quietly with his face in his hands, trying to gather himself. Even Bryan needed a moment as he stood against the wall with tears in his eyes.

"Dang, bro, I know that was hard," observed Bryan.

"Yep, it was hard, real hard, but necessary. The forgiveness wasn't for him, but for me!

In order for my sins to be forgiven, I have to forgive him. Thank you, Lord, for Grace," Nigel prayed. Then, Bryan escorted him back to work.

Within months, Nigel made a full recovery. He felt as if his life was his again.

One night, Nigel received a call from his dad.

"Hello son, just a quick reminder about the cookout on Saturday night. Your grandpa's brother Virgil will be in town. Uncle Virgil is the last one of the lineage, pressing on at the ripe old age of 96. He hasn't been home in 40 years."

"Yes sir, we'll be there," Nigel promised.

It was now Saturday night and the Hendersons' driveway was full.

"How many people did your dad invite?" queried Monica.

"I don't know, but it looks like everyone with the Henderson last name." They both laughed.

As they entered the backyard, the family greeted them with joy. Most of them were still

flabbergasted at how well Nigel was doing.

"Come on son, bring the family. Let me introduce you guys to Uncle Virgil."

"Where is he?" asked Nigel.

"In the kitchen with the ladies," he responded.

"Uncle Virgil, this is my miracle boy!" announced his dad.

Nigel almost dropped the potato salad when the light brown-skinned, freckle-faced old man extended his wrinkled hand.

"What fine boys you have and the little one looks like me" said Uncle Virgil

Monica's heart smiled.

Made in the USA
Columbia, SC
24 July 2024

38626234R00074